Twilight of the Ice

Other Books by Harry Mark Petrakis

Novels

Lion at My Heart
The Odyssey of Kostas Volakis
A Dream of Kings
In the Land of Morning
The Hour of the Bell
Nick the Greek
Days of Vengeance
Ghost of the Sun

Short Story Collections

Pericles on 31st Street
The Waves of Night
A Petrakis Reader—27 Stories
Collected Stories

Memoirs and Essays

Stelmark—A Family Recollection
Reflections: A Writer's Life—A Writer's Work
Tales of the Heart

Biography and History

The Founder's Touch
Henry Crown: The Life and Times of the Colonel

TWILIGHT OF THE ICE

Harry Mark Petrakis

SOUTHERN ILLINOIS UNIVERSITY PRESS

Carbondale and Edwardsville

Printed in the United States of America

06 05 04 03 4 3 2 1

Library of Congress Cataloging-in-Publication Data

Petrakis, Harry Mark.
Twilight of the ice / Harry Mark Petrakis.
p. cm.
I. Title.
PS3566.E78 T87 2003
813'.54—dc21
ISBN 0-8093-2514-4 (alk. paper)
ISBN 0-8093-2506-3 (pbk. : alk. paper) 2002014558

Printed on recycled paper. ♻

The paper used in this publication meets the minimum requirements of American National Standard for Information Sciences—Permanence of Paper for Printed Library Materials, ANSI Z39.48-1992. ∞

Once again, for my wife, Diana,
who has shared and endured
our highs and our lows
for more than half a century,
and
for the late, great film director Sam Peckinpah,
who encouraged me to write this story

Twilight of the Ice

1

Mike

WHEN HE WOKE THAT MORNING IN MARCH, MIKE began slowly flexing his arms and legs under the covers. During sleep, his muscles had stiffened and his joints locked, and even after he'd gotten up, his soreness and pain lingered.

His pain on waking recalled the dyspeptic ice company doctor's diagnosis of his body's deterioration a few weeks earlier.

"You got scar tissue all over your body." The doctor's gloomy face studied Mike's file. "A broken arm in 1937, a dislocated shoulder in '45, a torn Achilles tendon in '49 . . . that was less than a year ago."

"Accidents happen when you're icing," Mike brusquely interrupted the bleak recital. "Rain and snow make the catwalks slippery, or maybe a train moves without warning. You work on a HiLift truck, you got to expect a few falls and breaks."

The doctor ignored his explanation.

"How long you been icing now?"

"Thirty years next month."

"That's too long to be working the trucks," the doctor frowned. "Your fractures and the wear and tear on your body have caused extensive degeneration. The tendons and muscles in your shoulders and knees are rotting away."

"Hell, Doc, only my shoulders and knees?" Mike cried. "I'm

damn glad my head and feet aren't rotting too!" His sarcasm was lost on the joyless sawbones.

"My advice is you better think seriously about giving up the icing," the doctor said somberly. "Even if you quit now, your condition will probably keep getting worse."

Apparently satisfied at the neatness of his diagnosis, the doctor looked past Mike toward the anteroom where his next patient waited.

If I'm going to rot whether I work or not, why should I quit, Mike thought indignantly outside the doctor's office. Through the decades he'd been icing, his work had provided him challenge and fulfillment. He had been lucky in starting at a time when the great icemen, Israel and Pacheco, worked the HiLift trucks. They took uncommon pride in their calling, a pride they had fostered in him.

Now Pacheco was dead and Israel retired years ago. Mike wasn't fool enough to think he could go on forever. He knew a day would come when he'd no longer be able to work. Yet, in spite of the doctor's grim assessment, he felt that his retirement was still years away.

From the hallway outside his apartment, someone knocked timidly on his door. He tossed aside his covers, pushed himself off the bed, and hobbled around barefooted to loosen his muscles and forestall cramps. Pulling on his cotton robe, he limped to open the door. His neighbor, Mrs. Danolas, a thin-faced woman in her forties, stood in the hallway.

"I'm sorry to bother you, Mr. Zervakis," she said nervously, "but you can tell we got almost no heat again. The children are eating lunch in their coats. Could you talk to Mr. Cordoba once more? He only seems to listen to you."

"I'll talk to him, Mrs. Danolas," Mike said firmly. "I'll go see him as soon as I'm dressed."

After closing the door, he exhaled and saw the vapor of his breath. He put his hand on the frigid metal of the radiator, and for the fourth or fifth time that winter, he cursed the greedy landlord in the basement apartment.

He carried his anger into the bathroom, where his battered visage stared at him from the cracked vanity mirror—sun-blackened complexion, cheeks a spiderweb of wrinkles, unruly gray hair, and dark, deep-set eyes.

"You're not only getting older and more crippled, you bastard," he muttered at his reflection, "you're getting uglier too."

He shaved and patted an astringent lotion on his cheeks. Afterwards, he dressed before the bureau that held an old browned photograph of his mother and sister back in their village in Crete. There was another photograph, of President Harry Truman, a man Mike admired for his spunk and straight talk. In the hallway, after he'd dressed, he pulled on his bulky fleece jacket and cap and started down the stairs.

The old building in which he lived was a bazaar of nations, with forty apartments, ten on each floor. The corridors and stairwells were filled with the sharp aromas of varied ethnic foods, while shrill snatches of Spanish, Greek, and Italian carried through the doors.

On the second floor, a baby's wail from one of the apartments reminded him of the children in the building. That further inflamed his anger against the landlord.

He'd moved into his apartment fifteen years earlier. The ownership of the building had changed four times since then, each owner more avaricious than the ones who had come before. Many of the tenants were newly arrived Greek immigrants who had difficulty making their complaints in English, and they turned to Mike for help. He became the Greek tenants' defender and, little by little, was conscripted as advocate for the other residents as well. It wasn't a role he sought, but he accepted it resolutely, feeling the cause of the tenants to be just.

Mike cajoled the owners into making needed repairs and improvements and when those flatteries failed, he used thinly veiled threats. Only once had he actually resorted to violence, with an owner who was an Anatolian Turk. Goaded by ancient enmities between Greek and Turk, after one bitter confrontation when he'd learned the Turk planned to evict a Greek family that had fallen behind in their rent, Mike lost his temper and kicked the owner down a flight of stairs. The Turk wasn't seriously hurt, and perhaps a shred of remorse about his predatory treatment of the tenants prevented him from pressing battery charges against Mike. Not long after that, however, possibly deciding that Mike would remain a constant obstacle to his dreams of profit, the Turk had sold the building.

Before the basement apartment of the current landlord, who was almost as heartless as the Turk, Mike knocked briskly on the door. Mrs. Cordoba opened it, her face suddenly pale when she saw him.

"Hello, Mr. Zervakis," she said, her voice trembling. "If you're looking for Leonard, he's not . . . I mean I think he might have gone out."

"Would you mind checking again, Mrs. Cordoba?" Mike asked quietly. "If I don't see him now, I'll have to keep coming back."

She peered nervously at him and then retreated with quick, tense steps into the adjoining room. Mike heard her husband's hissing voice berating her. A moment later, the obese figure of the landlord came hesitantly toward the hallway.

"I know you're here about the heat, Mr. Zervakis," Cordoba said warily. "I'm sorry the furnace broke again . . . the repairman is on the—"

Mike grasped the man by his beefy arm and pulled him into the hallway. With his other hand he closed the apartment door so the landlord's wife wouldn't hear.

"You penny-squeezing scrap of shit!" Mike said in a low, harsh voice. "I warned you last month about cutting down the heat! You got babies and small children in the building! You want them all sick?"

"The furnace broke!" Cordoba said shrilly. "It's not my fault!"

"Listen to me," Mike went on grimly. "I'm going out. When I get back, if there isn't heat, not just a little heat, but heat rushing through the radiators all the way up to the fourth floor, I'm going to kick your fat, greedy ass out into the street! Do you understand?"

The terrified landlord nodded, and when Mike let him go, he scurried back into the apartment.

Mike knew the miser hadn't been cured of his stinginess. He'd raise the thermostat for a while until greed unbalanced him once more. Since his own apartment was located beside the furnace room, a minimum of heat was enough to keep his own fat shanks warm. His wife, a decent, timid woman, was too frightened of her husband to oppose him.

Mike walked out of the building, pulling his collar up against the raw midday air. Rain had fallen earlier and would probably fall again by the time he had to leave for work. Cars and trucks rumbled through the puddles on Halsted Street, horns honked, an ambulance passed with its siren wailing. Filtered through the moist air was the stench of slaughtered animals carried on the wind from the stockyards further south.

A month earlier, in mid-February, snow had fallen across the city, white when it fell but then becoming black slush because of the cinders and pollution. The thaw was followed by a few mild days, and then a bone-chilling cold returned. Now, in the middle of March, the city remained battered between periods of snow and freezing rain.

Sometimes, in the coldest, darkest part of a Chicago winter, Mike thought nostalgically of the sun of his family's homeland of Crete. He had left the island as a boy to come to America, but he still remembered playing nearly naked in the sustaining heat of the sun.

That sun was his only happy memory of Crete. During his childhood, the island had still been under Turkish rule, so the Cretans, in addition to their poverty, were forced to endure the cruelty of their Turkish masters. In their village, Mike, his father, his mother, and his sister had been at the mercy of any Turk who chose to abuse them. As a child Mike saw villagers humiliated and beaten. There were also the times his sister, Marika, and he were hidden by their parents in the fruit cellar under their house when drunken Turks rampaged through his village. He would never forget the terror he felt then, huddled and trembling beside his crying sister.

In 1910, when Mike (he'd been christened Manolis) was fourteen years old, his Uncle Apostolos, who had gone to America some years earlier and opened a restaurant, offered to pay the steerage fares to bring Mike and his sister to America. Marika was too young to leave their parents, but Mike was eager to see the new world. He didn't learn until later that his uncle's motives weren't an unselfish concern for the welfare of his nephew but to use Mike for menial labor in his business.

When Mike arrived in Chicago, he went to work at once in the kitchen of what his uncle's letters had referred to as a restaurant but what was in reality an unsavory lunchroom in a factory district. Through breakfast, lunch, and dinner, Mike washed dishes in the battered iron tub. He also swept the floors, scoured the pots, and unloaded the crates of produce and canned goods from the delivery trucks.

In return for his nearly eighty hours of labor a week, his uncle paid Mike's rent in a cockroach-riddled rooming house occupied by new immigrants. Mike ate his meals in the lunchroom and received fifty cents a week. Even that paltry sum was paid to him grudgingly, his uncle whining about all the money he was sending to Mike's family in Crete. Mike knew the sum was considerably less than he would have sent if he were being paid a decent wage.

His uncle justified his miserliness by repeatedly reassuring Mike that since there were no other heirs, someday he might inherit the business. Mike suspected his uncle was lying, but even if he had been telling the truth, any prospect of inheriting the lunchroom filled him with revulsion.

As he grew from childhood to manhood, Mike looked on his years in the lunchroom as a lonely, unhappy period of unrelenting drudgery. Since his uncle hadn't allowed him time off to go to school or to meet other young people, the only redeeming experience of those years was that he'd learned to read and write English from a compassionate old cook in the lunchroom who pitied him. During quiet hours when his uncle was away buying meat and produce, the cook tutored Mike in grammar and vocabulary. From time to time, that good man also brought him a few books, which Mike read over and over and treasured.

In one of his sister's letters from the village, Mike learned that Crete had finally been liberated from the Turks. A year later she wrote that his father had been killed fighting in the Macedonian campaign in the Balkan War. His own wretchedness left Mike little energy to mourn his dead father.

On those infrequent times when he wrote to his sister and his mother, he was ashamed to tell them about his uncle's deception. He lied and wrote that he was doing well, making a place for himself in America.

During the years he worked for his uncle, Mike came to loathe the man's avarice and meanness. He also despised everything about the lunchroom—the smells of spoiled food, the grease floating on the dishwater, the patrons who grunted like animals as they gorged down their food.

Mike continued to work in the kitchen twelve hours a day, six and a half days a week, all through the First World War. When he wasn't working, he spent his time sleeping to combat his exhaustion and depression. About the war itself, he knew little beyond what he heard from lunchroom customers talking of trench warfare and battlefields with French and German names.

In early November 1918, an eruption of firecrackers and horns heralded the news that the war was over and the Allies had won. Everyone in the lunchroom ran into the street to cheer and celebrate, and Mike left the kitchen sink to shout and clap with them. For the first time in years, he felt lighthearted and hopeful even as the euphoria of the victory reminded him of his own miserable existence. He vowed to free himself from bondage, as well, and that evening he told his uncle he was quitting the kitchen. That wasn't enough to satisfy his pent-up anger and resentment, and he denounced the lunchroom as a cesspool only fit to serve pigs.

Uncle Apostolos was shocked. His voice trembling with anger and outrage, he ranted that Greeks and restaurants were bonded like blood and bone.

"Without restaurants, we Greeks could never have survived!" his uncle cried. "We would be no better than Gypsies, wandering from place to place, rootless and homeless! We came to this country, unable to speak the language, locked out of jobs and businesses by those who came before! Restaurants became our salvation in America! For a Greek to curse a restaurant is like spitting on the holy church!"

Finally, his uncle called Mike ungrateful and disloyal and predicted he'd come crawling back begging for his job washing dishes. Mike assured him he'd die first.

Since he was without any savings, Mike had to find work at once. A lunchroom patron suggested he try the stockyards. Mike applied and did get a job. After his first day of work, he was shocked at the perversity of fate that had hurled him from a cesspool into a bloody world of slaughter.

The stockyards ran from Thirty-ninth to Forty-seventh Street, a network of connected buildings and railroad cars holding thousands of hogs, cows, and sheep waiting to be slaughtered. Afterwards, the carcasses were severed into cuts of meat, while the inedible parts were converted into soap and fertilizer.

The worst thing about the yards was the pervasive stench, and in his first week, Mike felt a number of times that he was going to vomit. The stink was most intense on the killing floor and in the slaughtering compounds.

There was also a constant danger of injury. Hardly a week passed without one or more workers getting cut by the sharp knives used to carve meat or having their fingers crushed in the chains and conveyer belts that carried the meat from one work station to the next. On the loading docks where Mike worked, there were fewer accidents, but the pace was hectic and relentless.

He would have quit at the end of his first week but feared he might not find another job. He stuck it out and for the first time since coming to America, had a little money in his pocket. In this time, he lived in a room in a run-down tenement in Bridgeport, a city neighborhood adjoining the stockyards. A small kerosene heater provided him heat, and his hot water came from a tea kettle he kept on top of the heater. Yet he didn't mind living frugally because every payday he was able to send money to his mother and sister in Crete.

Meanwhile, the stockyards provided him his first lesson in democracy. He had to work with Bohemian, Lithuanian, and Polish immigrants as well as with black men from the farms of Mississippi and Georgia.

In the beginning, still harboring the distrust people in his village felt toward strangers, he was wary and suspicious of everyone. In time he learned to assess a man by how well he did his work and how fairly he treated others. Yet he was also thankful that among all the workers of varied backgrounds, he had never encountered a Turk where his new tolerance might be sorely tested.

He'd worked in the yards almost two years when one afternoon he saw two men transferring blocks of ice from the elevated platform of a truck into the bunkers of a railroad meat car. He had seen men icing cars before, but this crew was different. One was a tall giant of a man, and the other was shorter but stocky and powerfully built. Mike was awed at the agility and strength the men displayed as they balanced like acrobats on the roofs of the cars and at the swiftness and ease with which they handled the huge blocks of ice. They seemed to him strong and towering figures like those he'd read about in the myths of Greece.

The following day, as he was finishing his shift, Mike saw that crew icing again, and he spoke to the men about his chances of getting work. The giant whose name was Israel Sullivan and his partner, Pacheco Juarez, seemed to understand the fascination Mike felt for the icing. They let him ride with them back to their depot and recommended him to the work boss as a strong and eager applicant. Mike was hired, and that was how he'd begun icing thirty years earlier.

Mike dug his hands deeper into the pockets of his jacket, flexing his cold fingers to warm them. He crossed Roosevelt Road, walked south to Fourteenth, and turned onto Maxwell Street.

In the stockyards, he'd worked alongside a man who had sailed as a young seaman on a freighter that made ports in the Arctic. He told Mike of visiting Eskimo tribes that lived on ice floes so isolated there was nothing around their solitary settlements for hundreds of miles but bears and seals.

At the opposite end of the world from that Arctic habitat was Maxwell Street with its bustling traders' market and its hundreds of vendors, pushcarts, and stalls. Mike enjoyed the vitality of the street, as integral a part of Chicago as the stockyards, and the astonishing diversity of people who came to haggle and trade. There were Orthodox Jews in wide-brimmed black hats and long caftans mingling with ruddy-cheeked Irish dandies and olive-complected Italians and Greeks. There were American Indians wearing beaded, feathered headbands and blonde-haired, light-eyed Scandinavians, and Gypsy women with rings and bracelets dangling from their ears and wrists.

Mike pushed deeper into the brawl of the crowd, passing poultry stalls with scrawny chickens in wire cages and butcher booths that reminded him of the stockyards with the chunks of raw meat hanging on hooks, dripping blood into the street. There were also ready-to-eat foods, fish stews and chicken soups, boiling ham shanks and skewers of sizzling beef. Mingling with all these aromas was another city smell he had come to know well, the stink of garbage burning in the trash barrels.

A little after two o'clock, Mike walked beneath the faded sign of the Santorini Bar and down a short flight of stairs. He entered a dimly lit basement room toasted by the aroma of brandies and rank cigars.

Leonidas Simis, the owner, short, stocky, and with a thick mustache, greeted Mike heartily. He motioned brusquely toward a shadowed alcove.

"The old Minotaur is already here, Mike," he said. "I'll bring you brandy and coffee right away."

Mike took off his jacket and cap as he walked to the corner table to join Israel, the giant he had first seen icing at the stockyards thirty years earlier. The old iceman, grown grizzled and white haired, sat musing over his brandy. When Israel saw Mike, a warm smile illuminated his face. As Mike clasped the iceman's huge hand, he felt the gnarled fingers and swollen knuckles of the crippling arthritis that had ended Israel's icing.

"Sorry I'm late, Israel," Mike said. "I'm having more and more trouble dragging my dead ass out of bed."

"Waiting for you gave me time to sit and ponder my life," Israel said. "I wondered what the world would gain if I stayed around a little longer? Then again, what would the world lose if I departed?"

"For one thing, Israel, I'd miss you a hell of a lot," Mike said. "And so would all those people you preach to in church. For all our sakes, Israel, try to stick around."

Leonidas brought Mike a brandy and a cup of steaming black coffee.

"Put it on my bill," Israel told the owner.

"No charge for Mike," Leonidas said brusquely. "A friend drinks free in the Santorini."

"I thought I was your friend too."

"Everyone who comes in here to drink is my friend.

"Then why don't I drink free?"

"Only my Greek friends drink free. All the times you come in here, preacher, you should know that."

"Its still blatant prejudice!" Israel scowled at the owner. "Bigotry too!"

"Prejudice? Bigotry?" Leonidas said indignantly. "It's geography! Mike and me come from Greece, and my Greek friends drink free!"

"If you continue that intolerant, bigoted attitude," Israel growled, "I'll take my business elsewhere."

"Suit yourself, preacher," Leonidas said crisply. "I'm not getting rich on your brandy and coffee."

"Put Israel's brandy and coffee on my tab," Mike laughed. "I got to pay for something."

The owner moved away.

"The truth is, this musty bar is probably as good a place for us to be as any other," Israel said. "Do you realize, my friend, we're here drinking at the crossroads of existence? Within a few blocks of this unsanctified basement are brothels that serve the assorted hungers of men, churches that heal and forgive their sins, and, finally, a hospital where mortals can die in an antiseptic environment."

Mike admired Israel's vision and his expansive flights of language. What made him even more amazing was that the old iceman, the seventh son of a Jewish mother and Irish father, was self-taught, his education achieved by a love for reading and books. Sometimes Mike had difficulty understanding the things Israel spoke about, but the preacher often provided him insight into people and life.

"You're forgetting the Team Track," Mike said, "That belongs to this crossroads too."

"Ay, the Team Track!" Israel said gravely. "That scabby, forlorn scrap of earth where we work, as sacred to us icemen as Athens is to the Greeks and Jerusalem to the Jews. You're right, I mustn't forget the Team Track."

He paused and peered intently across the table at Mike.

"I had a dream about you last night, Mike," Israel said. "I was holding a revival at the mission and you were seated in the congregation. When I called witnesses for Jesus, you were the first man to step forward." He sighed. "God be praised, it was a glorious moment."

"Now, Israel, you know I'm not the kind to jump up like some holy roller and claim I found religion," Mike said. "I think sometimes you get so carried away by the power of your preaching, you mix me up with another iceman."

"Even in a dream I'd know your rocky, weather-battered head," Israel said. "It was you! Pacheco and Abrogano were there too."

"Most preachers would be satisfied, Israel, preaching to the living," Mike said. "You got to bring the dead back into your congregation, as well."

"That was the beauty of the revelation!" Israel exclaimed.

"Two dead icemen returned from purgatory to witness a prodigal find Jesus! It was a miracle!"

"I admire your faith, Israel," Mike said, "and I know you're a powerful dreamer. But I got to walk my own road."

"Walk with Jesus and the road won't be as hard!" Israel said fervently. "I've told you many times before, he'll help you fathom your place in the crusade of the ice."

"And I've told you before, I don't know what icing has to do with a crusade," Mike said genially. "Icing is loading the trucks, hauling it to the trains, filling the bunkers with ice quickly, and doing it right. You iced enough years to understand that."

"The icing is the crusade!" Israel said fervently. "You're the only icemaster left now, Mike, the last champion. Before you put down your pick and tongs, you've got to find someone strong and talented you can teach your craft, someone to carry on the icing after you're gone!"

Israel's words rang with passion. He took another sip of brandy, his voice becoming quieter and more pensive.

"When I first started icing so many years ago," Israel said, "we were only a few years into this century. You should have seen the Team Track then. We hauled ice by horse-drawn carts and then used block and tackle to hoist it to the top of the cars. Mules and wagons delivered bread and milk, and elegant horse-drawn buggies carried the gentry around town. Many nights, Pacheco and I rode the empty wagon back to the Team Track and would see the lamplighter igniting the gas streetlamps. I never thought then that Pacheco would die, that I'd live to preach in my own church, someday have a fine iceman like you as a friend."

Israel leaned back in his chair and closed his eyes. A long, deep sigh passed his lips.

Mike studied Israel's granite face and majestic head. He loved and admired the old iceman he had worked with for two decades.

For a long time after he'd started to work, Mike retained the awe he felt when he first saw Israel and Pacheco icing. The two men worked in tandem so seamlessly that it seemed their bodies linked to one another and to the ice in a fluid, unbroken flow.

In the beginning, Mike despaired of ever being able to match their quickness and skill.

But they accepted him as a strong and earnest novice and took him under their tutelage. They worked him relentlessly, passing on to him their own knowledge of the ice. Mike made every effort to be an attentive and dutiful student. After the years he'd spent locked in the foul, humid air of the kitchen, the open air cleared and expanded his lungs, and the hard, daily labor increased his strength. Standing high on the catwalk of cars, he felt joyful and brimming with power.

After several years of hard work, watching and learning, Mike's ability approached the skill of his teachers. They were spare but fair in their praise, which meant a great deal to him. Finally, the day when he could hold his own on the HiLifts beside them was the day he felt reborn as a man.

Mike worked with the two veteran icemen for a dozen years. Then, one summer afternoon while they were at work icing a long train of produce cars at Proviso, Pacheco's lion heart collapsed. The iceman who had seemed so indestructible to Mike tumbled from the catwalk of a car to the earth. Men who were working nearby swore that when Pacheco's body landed on the ground, the earth shook as though a great tree struck by lightning had fallen.

The grief Mike felt at Pacheco's death was nothing compared to his partner's anguish. For months, Israel worked in a silent, driven fury, hurling and cutting the ice as if he too wished his belabored heart to falter so he might join his partner in death.

Then, less than a year after Pacheco's death, the arthritis that had for years begun to impair Israel's hands and joints suddenly grew worse. Soon afterwards, a day came when his crippled fingers couldn't hold the tongs, his joint-locked arms couldn't swing the pick. Israel was forced to give up the work he loved so much.

Still grieving for his friend, his own body failing, the old iceman slipped into a dark depression. For months he never left his small apartment and, during the day, kept the shades drawn to deflect any light. He lost his zest for life and his appetite for food. Mike brought him soup and bread and pleaded with Israel to eat. He watched helplessly as his friend grew weaker, seeming to drift closer to death.

Then, about six months after he ceased working on the trucks, another friend prevailed upon Israel to attend services at the Pacific Garden Mission Church of Blind Dobby. The eloquent, sightless old evangelist struck a fire in Israel. Almost overnight, the iceman achieved a miraculous recovery from his depression. In the following year, he became one of Blind Dobby's most fervent converts, from time to time preaching to the congregation himself. When the evangelist died, Israel replaced him as pastor to the street people who filled the mission. His sermons were explosive revelations of his new-found faith, and his church was crowded each time he preached.

Mike's reverie was broken by Israel's voice calling to Leonidas for another brandy.

"Oscar Kroner over at Capital Ice was telling me at the mission that they installed another one of those new icing machines at the Rock Island," Israel said.

Mike despised the huge, ugly machines that were beginning to appear in the yards. These machines carried the ice by conveyer belt to the top of the cars and then deposited the chunks automatically into the bunkers.

"That's the third one in the city this year," Mike said. "But some of the yardmasters are griping about them, telling us they don't always work . . . sometimes the pulleys and chains break."

"Even if they make them better," Israel said, "it'll be years before all the locations have them. And, God forbid, even when they use them in more and more yards, why there'll always be a place on the HiLifts for a good iceman."

Mike hoped fervently that Israel was right. The grim prospect that all truck and platform icing might become obsolete as a result of the machines made him angry and also filled him with an unsettling fear, as well.

"I've got a prayer meeting at the mission this evening," Israel said. "Why don't you drop by."

"Even if I wanted to come," Mike said," Earl's got me working nights."

"You've got more seniority than anyone at the Team Track!" Israel said sternly. "You shouldn't be working nights! Tell him you won't work!"

"I'll be damned before I ask the yahoo for anything," Mike shrugged. "In four, five weeks he'll begin hiring the summer crews. He'll have to put me on days then."

"He'll find other ways to torment you," Israel said grimly.

"I know you think Earl is one of the devil's disciples," Mike said. "Now, I got to admit he's one mean, oversized, and unhappy bastard. But if he's really the devil's messenger, there are more important places he could be doing his dirty work. Why would he be hanging out at the Team Track?"

"The Team Track is one of the battlegrounds!" Israel said sternly. "That's why Satan has chosen to send one of his disciples there!"

Those apocalyptic visions of crusade and of Satan that Israel spoke about so often confounded Mike. He shared the preacher's belief that he had inherited the legacy of the ice as a craft and that he was duty-bound to pass that skill on to another man. That much he and Israel believed. But Mike had difficulty comprehending the preacher's view of the survival of the ice as a struggle between God and the devil. At times Mike couldn't help feeling that perhaps all the travail the old iceman had endured had left him subject to apparitions that didn't really exist.

Israel seemed to have read Mike's thoughts. "You think I'm crazy, don't you?"

"I don't think you're crazy, Israel," Mike said earnestly. "I worked with you too long to believe that. But I don't remember you talking about crusades and Satan when we iced together on the HiLifts. All you cared about then was filling the bunkers quick as you could, doing the job better than anyone else."

"I hadn't found my way to God yet," Israel said. "I had to go down to hell and see Satan for myself, come close to having him destroy me, before I could find God's eye and understand the role he wanted me to play!"

Mike finished his brandy and rose to leave.

"All right, Israel," he said wryly, "every spur and yard where I ice, I'll be on the lookout for a devil with horns and a tail. But I got to tell you if I do see him, the shock might cause me to fall on my ass and break my damn neck."

"Satan's disciples don't always appear with horns, a pointed tail, and cloven hoofs," Israel said somberly. "They might take on the misshapen body of a creature such as Earl, who seeks to destroy the spirit of good men by his wickedness!"

"You must be talking about Turks," Leonidas said as he brought Israel another brandy.

"I'm talking about Lucifer, Satan, Old Nick, Old Scratch, Beelzebub, the devil!" Israel said fervently.

"It's the same thing," Leonidas said grimly. "Turks."

When Mike returned to his apartment, he was pleased to hear steam hissing in the radiators and the rooms well-heated. He ran water into the old four-legged tub and added a kettle of boiling water. He stripped and soaked, the water soothing his body. Afterwards, he slept for an hour. When he woke, twilight had fallen, and the neon glow from the Halsted Street shops and taverns flickered across his windows.

He opened a can of chicken soup and made a salami sandwich. In the middle of his meal, there was a light knock on his door. The ten-year-old daughter of Mrs. Danolas, a child with dark hair and large dark eyes, brought him a small tray of baklava.

"Mama says thank you for the heat," the little girl said gravely. Mike took the tray and smiled.

"Tell your mama I thank her."

After finishing his meal, he ate several pieces of the rich honey-nut dessert. He wrapped what was left to carry to Mendoza, his partner on the truck. Then it was time for him to go down to his car and drive to the team track for his night of work.

2

Rafer

RAFER FIRST CAME TO THE TEAM TRACK IN THE middle of March in 1950. The winter had been a harsh one, alternating periods of snow, cold, and freezing rain. Each morning his face reflected in the cracked mirror of the hotel bathroom had taken on more of the gray pallor of the sky.

He had just completed a three-week alcohol addiction program run by the Pacific Garden Mission. He came out dry and shaken, not certain he'd been cured of his longing for a drink and afraid that he might falter once again. He'd been through these programs several times in the past and knew each lapse brought him closer to the legion of lost drunks. These men huddled in doorways or in alleys, clutching pints of wine the way a mother holds her child. What provided him a little hope was that once before, after a sobriety program, he'd remained dry for almost three months.

Those first days after sobering were always the hardest. Every package liquor store was a lure to cheerfulness, every bar a threshold to euphoria.

To help the rehabilitated drunks escape the indolence that led to further entrapments, the Pacific Garden Mission posted lists of neighborhood jobs. Most were menial tasks, washing dishes in short-order lunchrooms or sweeping up in neighborhood bars. One of the jobs Rafer saw on the list was for a dispatcher at a location called the Team Track. The address was on South Fifteenth Street, a short stretch off Halsted and about two miles from the Poinsettia Hotel on Harrison Street where he had a cubicle with a washbasin and a cot.

Rafer had only a few dollars and sorely needed a job. Hoping to gain an edge on others who might apply, he started walking toward the location on the same rainy, windy night he first read the notice. He walked with his head bent against the cold rain and thought several times of turning back.

At Fifteenth Street, he turned off Halsted and started up the hill. Rainwater had flooded the ruts carved from the wheels of trucks, and within minutes, his shoes and socks were soaked. By the time he reached the cluster of buildings halfway up the hill, he was chilled to the bone.

The site appeared deserted until he saw several cars parked outside a small building with a light pole in front and a single lighted window. As he walked beneath the bare-bulbed light suspended over the door, a swarm of pigeons roosting on the pole above the light took flight with a noisy flurry of wings.

Rafer peered through the window into a small office and saw an old man seated at a desk. He moved to the door and knocked. When there wasn't any answer, he knocked a second time.

"W'at you want?" The old man's voice carried tensely through the door.

"I'm here for the dispatcher job," Rafer spoke loudly.

"No one here for hirin' now! Come back in the mornin' af'er six!"

"I walked up here in the rain," Rafer said urgently. "Can you let me in a couple minutes to warm up?"

There was a long pause before the door was unlocked and then opened a crack. The old man peered out nervously.

"If you lookin' for money," he said, "I ain' got a dime."

"I'm just looking for a job," Rafer said.

The old man was in his late sixties or early seventies, slight-bodied with matted gray hair and a pinched, sullen face.

As Rafer reached to pull off his hat, the old man stepped back warily. Rafer imagined the sight he made. A rain-soaked vagrant in his middle forties who looked in his fifties, his face drawn and wasted, his tousled dark hair showing streaks of gray. He knew he wasn't a figure to inspire trust.

"This ain' no time to come lookin' for any job," the old man snapped. "You s'posed to come in the mornin' and see the straw boss. He ain' here 'til six."

"Other guys will come looking for the job in the morning," Rafer said, "and I need work real bad." He motioned toward the stove. "All right if I warm up?"

Without waiting for the old man's consent, Rafer walked to the stove, stretching his cold fingers as near the cast iron surface as he could without getting burned.

In addition to the pot-bellied stove, the office held several battered wooden desks, a few chairs, and a cluster of telephones. There was a hot plate with a small pot of coffee on the burner and a shelf with mugs. A chipped file cabinet lodged in a corner.

"You din' need to break your neck gettin' here." The old man continued to watch him. "This job ain' not'in' special."

"What work do you do here?"

"This is an ice depot."

"You deliver ice to houses?"

"Naw, we don' deal in two-bit stuff like t'at," the old man scoffed. "Our boys haul four-hundred-pound blocks of ice by HiLift truck to the railroad yards. They load the ice into bunkers of freight cars t'at haul potatoes and ot'er vegetables and fruit."

"What does the dispatcher do?"

"You jes' take calls from the yardmasters and relay 'em to your crews," the old man said. "Firs', you got to learn the yards so's you know wha' crews to send."

He moved closer to the stove and peered sharply at Rafer. "You don' look so good to me," he said. "You ain' sick, are you? If you are, don' expect Earl to hire you." He paused. "Earl's the straw boss. He runs the Team Track."

"I'm not sick," Rafer said. "I'll be all right when I warm up."

A gust of wind swept the frame building and rattled the window and door. Rafer thought unhappily about trudging back through the cold, wet night.

"I walked a couple of miles here from Harrison Street," he said. "I'm wet and cold. How about letting me bunk here until morning?"

"Jesus Chris'!" the old man erupted in outrage. "I let you in so's you can warm up and you wanna stay all night! Earl don' like strangers roun' the place! He's strict on that!"

"I'd be up early, before he comes in," Rafer pleaded. "That way I could be first to see him too. I'm broke, mister, and I really need the job."

The old man glowered at him.

"All righ', all righ'!" he said finally, resentfully. "I'm tellin' you, Earl sees you been sleeping here, he'll raise hell with bot' of us!"

"I'll get up whenever you say."

The old man continued to stare at him indignantly. "An' don' t'ink you gonna sleep in here. You use the locker room. It's got benches an' a stove."

Rafer thanked him and walked through a small hallway into the locker room. Between the long twin rows of lockers were several benches. There was a pot-bellied wood-burning stove in one corner, and at the far end of the room, an alcove led into a toilet.

Rafer tugged off his coat and slumped wearily on the bench nearest the stove. He took off his shoes and spread his wet socks over the end of the bench to dry. He stretched his chilled feet close to the stove, feeling the heat ripple up his legs. After a few moments, the chill and trembling slowly left his body.

The old man shuffled into the locker room and sat down on a bench across from Rafer.

"I din' mean to yell like t'at," he said apologetically. "I ain' a bad guy . . . but you don' know what Earl's like if you break his rules." He leaned forward and put out his hand. "My name's Benjamin Tipton. The guys all call me Benny."

Rafer clasped the man's bony hand. "I'm Rafer Martin," he said.

Benny shook his hand limply and settled back on the bench. "You better know t'is job ain' no prize. I been here eight years now, and my belly's always in knots, an' I gotta hit the can t'ree, four times a night."

"Is the work that hard?"

"It ain' the work!" Benny said earnestly. "It's Earl!" He clenched his bony fists and waved them balefully in the air. "It ain' only he's big as a gorilla, but he's mean . . . I mean rattle-snake mean!" Rafer sensed the fear and loathing in the old man's voice. "I been roun' an' I worked for guys who were tough. But Earl . . . hones' to God, he makes you feel you no better than a cockroach or a worm. Know what I mean? Sometimes I feel I jes' can't take no more and I wanna quit . . . but jobs ain' easy for an old guy." He paused. "I jes' made some coffee. You wanna cup?"

"That'd be great." Rafer started to rise, but Benny waved him down. He walked into the office and returned with a mug of coffee.

"You ain' a commie organizer, are you?" Benny handed Rafer the mug. "Earl hates commies like poison. We had one guy here 'bout a year ago passing out commie leaflets. While he was talkin' to a few of our guys, someone—I ain' saying who—set his car on fire. He's one commie ain' never comin' back."

"I don't believe in the communist philosophy."

"I din' t'ink you did, but I figured I better ask." Benny paused. "Where you from?"

"I been living most of my life in California."

"How long you been in the windy city?"

"I rode in on a freight from Kansas City just after Christmas."

"Don' tell Earl you travel that way," Benny frowned. "If he t'inks you're a hobo goin' to hop a freight out of town in a couple weeks, you ain' gettin' the job."

"I'm planning to settle in the city here for a while."

"If you get the job, and if you can put up with Earl, you might jes' take my place," Benny said gloomily. "I don' t'ink I'll be 'roun too much longer."

"I wouldn't want to take your job."

"Ain' got not'in' to do with you," Benny said. "Only reason Earl keeps me 'roun so's he can make my life hell. One day he's gonna tell me I'm too old and can me. Don' mean not'in' to him." He scratched a mole on his cheek. "This time of year, the work ain' that hard."

Another surge of wind shook the building. Rafer felt grateful to be inside.

"We only got one crew working tonigh'," Benny said, "an' only six men on the payroll, eight if you coun' Salvatore, the truck mechanic, and me." Benny shivered. "Gettin' cold in here."

He walked to pick up a log from a woodpile in the corner and heaved it into the stove.

"Part of my job is keepin' the stoves going," Benny said. "Earl raises hell in the mornin' if the fires ain' burnin'." He slumped back on the bench. "Works hardest in summer," he said. "Startin' in May, Earl hires t'irty, forty more guys so's by June, we got twenty crews. Mos' stay 'til October. Weat'er turns cold, icing slows down, an' drifters and farmers take off. If I was younger, I'd go too."

The phone rang in the office and Benny hurried to answer.

Rafer walked to the toilet behind the locker room, which was damp with the trapped smells of urine and disinfectant. In addition to the urinals and stalls, there were several large cast-iron tubs.

Rafer shivered as he stepped with his bare feet into a puddle of cold water on the floor. At the same time, he caught a flash of an animal he took to be a rat scurrying for the shadows. He stood warily at the urinal, uneasily watching for another sign of the rat.

On the wall above the urinals were a pair of dog-eared signs. One scrawled message read DON'T PISS ON THE FLOOR. The other was labeled HOW YOU CAN SURVIVE: STEPS TO TAKE TO ESCAPE THE BOMB. Across the instructions someone had scribbled, "Bomb this place first!"

"A yardmaster callin' for ice," Benny told him after Rafer returned to the locker room. "I phone our guys icin' at Proviso so's they make the call, an' t'en they come in an' unload any ice left into the big house. If you gonna work here, you better know Earl's strict as hell 'bout leavin' ice on the truck."

"Will you get into trouble if they find me here?"

"Naw," Benny said. "Mike Zervakis and Luis Mendoza work year-round and are stan'-up guys. Mendoza, he's Mexican, and Mike, well, he's the only Greek I ever seen don' work in a rest'rant."

Benny shook his head earnestly.

"Mike's been here longer than anyone. Nex' to me, he's the oldes' guy here, but nobody ain' askin' Mike his age. A lot of stronger, younger guys come t'rough here, but nobody cuts and t'rows the ice like Mike." He gestured toward the office. "An' Mike's the only guy at the Team Track ain' afraid of Earl and stands up to him. Everyone else is scared of the bastard. You get the job, you see what I mean."

Benny rose and motioned to the bench.

"Better sleep now 'cause I'm wakin' you early." Benny took the mug. "I'm gonna grab forty winks myself."

After Benny left the locker room, Rafer moved closer to the stove. He remembered the rat and raised his feet to the bench and drew his coat over his legs. Another gust of wind rattled the windows, and he wished suddenly he had a drink.

He tried to distract that craving by thinking of his wife, Mellie, and their daughter, Rosalie, living in Los Angeles. He hadn't seen them now in more than a year.

When he and Mellie had married ten years earlier, he had already been battling the bottle. She hoped that by her loving efforts, he could be cured. For the first two years, he managed to stay sober. In that time, Mellie had become pregnant and delivered a baby girl they called Rosalie, after Rafer's mother, who'd died when he was a child.

Those first months after the baby's birth were the happiest Rafer had ever known. He taught high school in Los Angeles and after school, hurried home to his family.

One of the counselors in the addiction program asked him why, after two years of staying sober, he had begun drinking again.

Rafer wasn't sure, but he knew some of it had to do with the outbreak of war. Although he had a deferment because of his family, he had friends who were fighting and dying, and he felt he was letting them down.

Without telling Mellie, he tried to enlist and was rejected because of a tubercular lung he'd suffered as a child. He grew nervous and depressed, and that worried Mellie. In an effort to lighten his mood, on his way home from school one afternoon, he stopped in a bar for a quick shot. He had a second drink, and when he got home, he was more cheerful than he'd been in weeks.

But in the days and weeks that followed, when he continued to stop in the bar after school, there wasn't any way he could conceal his drinking. Seeing Mellie's growing despair and fear filled him with guilt and remorse. Those feelings drove him to drink even more.

His cravings grew stronger. He'd stop for a few days and then have nights when he'd wake at three or four in the morning, his body sweating and trembling, his throat so parched he felt he'd choke unless he had a drink.

He and Mellie talked endlessly, planned and schemed, vowed and prayed. He went several times to an AA meeting and for a few weeks felt the warmth and understanding of others who had been addicted. They helped him "white-knuckle it," that fist clenching effort needed to stop drinking. But each of those periods of good fellowship ended with another drinking spree.

The war ended, and when the veterans who had been teachers returned, Rafer was fired from his position at the high school. He began tutoring students on the side. The income wasn't sufficient, and Mellie had to go to work as a sales clerk in a neighborhood clothing store. They wouldn't have survived if it hadn't been for her parents who helped them financially.

He understood the destruction he was inflicting on his family and tried desperately to stop drinking. When he did manage to stay dry for a while, he experienced symptoms of withdrawal—nausea, sweating, trembling, and a tormenting anxiety that pursued him like a fury from room to room. At those times, the thought of suicide coiled like a snake in his heart.

In his drunken stupors, he suffered cuts and bruises and, when he passed out and fell, cracked lips and a gash in his forehead.

Then one terrible night, he was struck by an attack of bleeding. Blood ran from under his fingernails, from his mouth, and from his eyes. Mellie called for help and an ambulance came and transported Rafer to the hospital. He was sure he was going to die, and he wept for the waste of his life and for what would become of his wife and daughter.

But he survived. When he came out of intensive care, the grim-faced doctor informed him that he had hemorrhaged internally, a lethal bleeding that could return and kill him as his body succumbed to alcohol disease and liver failure.

For almost a year after that episode, terror kept him sober. Mellie and he slept together, and he drew strength from her devotion and love.

But his craving returned. At night, he'd wake bathed in sweat, his stomach knotted, his legs trembling. He got up and paced the rooms, his frenzy growing, convinced if he didn't get a drink he'd go mad. There was nothing to drink in the house, and he was about to sip some rubbing alcohol diluted in grape juice and then remembered a bottle he'd hidden in the garage. He retrieved it and sat in his car, gulping down one swallow after another. Mellie found him in a drunken stupor in the morning, the car reeking of whiskey.

In his desperation, he began to think that his only hope of saving himself for his family was to leave his family.

Mellie couldn't understand why he had to leave, but Rafer was convinced there wasn't any other way. He'd move his wife and daughter in with her parents who would care for them. Rafer would leave Los Angeles and begin a solitary journey to battle his demons. If he conquered them, he'd return to his family. If he couldn't beat them, Mellie and Rosie would be better off without him.

Yet he wasn't sure whether that was the real reason he was leaving or whether he wanted to be able to drink without having to listen to Mellie pleading for him to stop.

For a year, Rafer wandered across the country. When he was sober, he found menial work and lived in small, furnished rooms. During his drinking bouts, he slept in flophouses, his nightmares merging with the moans of other afflicted men around him.

In whatever city he resided, he wrote letters to Mellie, reporting on his progress, trying to reassure her that he hoped he'd earn the right to return home to his family. When he remained in one place for a while, he gave Mellie an address where she could write him. In the course of that year, he collected a dozen of her letters and photos of Rosie that he treasured.

He was sober in Minneapolis for a month and then lapsed. In Kansas City, he didn't drink for three weeks while he worked as a dishwasher. He spent two months in Detroit, working for a taxi company as a dispatcher. Fleeing the urge to begin drinking again, he left that city for Chicago and started drinking as soon as he got off the freight. In Chicago, at the Pacific Garden Mission, where he had a dormitory bed, he met a counselor, a compassionate man whose sad face bore the marks of his own torment. He convinced Rafer to enter the alcohol addiction program at the mission.

In the midst of his reveries, he must have fallen asleep, and the banging of a metal locker door startled him awake. He opened his eyes to see two men clad in bulky jackets and knit woolen caps standing at the lockers across from him. One of them gestured at Rafer.

"Didn't mean to scare you, friend." The man had a low, resonant voice.

Rafer rose awkwardly from the bench. "I'm here for the dispatcher job."

"Benny told us," the man said. "I'm Mike and long-legs here is Mendoza."

"I'm Rafer."

"Now that we met formally, Rafer," Mendoza smiled, "I got to tell you I think you're a little nuts." He tugged off his cap to reveal a bandanna tied at a rakish angle above his dark-complected face. "Why in hell would you want to work in this asshole of the city?"

"I need the job."

"Don't we all," Mendoza sighed.

The men tugged off their jackets. Mendoza had a lean, strong frame. Mike was shorter with thick graying hair, a powerful neck, and a deep-chested, iron-hard-looking body. But it was the iceman's face that was unlike any Rafer had ever seen. His forehead and cheeks were webbed with creases and wrinkles, his skin so weathered and darkened by sun and wind that his face seemed carved from the bark of a tree.

The two men walked to the toilet, and Rafer heard water splashing in the iron tubs. Although his socks were still wet, he pulled them on and slipped into his shoes. The men returned to the locker room and picked up their jackets.

"We're going down to Halsted for some chow," Mendoza said. "If you fall asleep again, man, best be up before the fat man comes in. He'll have your liver for breakfast."

"Benny will wake you before Earl gets in," Mike said. "I hope you get the job."

They left the locker room and exchanged a few words with Benny, Mendoza needling the old man about his coffee. The office door slammed closed.

Rafer put another log into the stove. He lay back down on the bench but couldn't sleep. There wasn't any sound from the office, and he feared Benny might have fallen asleep. He remained wakeful and tense, listening to the wind and to the wood crackling in the stove until he heard Benny's quick steps. The old man entered the locker room, tugging urgently at his belt, and hurried past him to the toilet.

When he returned from the toilet, he paused at the bench. "You gotta get up now. I'm gonna tell Earl you come in jes' a few minutes 'fore him. You back me up."

Rafer washed his face at one of the tubs and carried his coat and hat into the office. With each moment that passed, Benny grew more anxious.

"Remember now," Benny said," I'm tellin' Earl you jes' got in. An' we gotta put more wood in the stoves. I'll get t'is one and you can handle the stove in the locker room. Earl likes it warm."

Rafer carried logs from the corner and threw them into the stove. He returned to the office.

They sat in silence while Benny kept looking nervously at the clock on the wall. Rafer absorbed some of the old man's fear, his stomach churning.

The sky was still dark when the rumbling of a car carried into the office. Benny fumbled at the side of his desk.

"Buzzer here opens the garage door so's Earl can park inside."

Rafer listened to the garage door creaking open and the noise of a car entering. After a brief silence, a car door slammed. Even before the straw boss entered the office, Rafer felt the floorboards creaking under the man's weight.

He expected to see a big man, but he was still shocked at Earl's size. The straw boss loomed three to four inches over six feet, with a massive, shapeless body that almost totally blocked the doorway. He walked slowly and heavily into the office, his weight causing his shoes to scrape along the floor.

When Earl passed under the light, Rafer saw his broad, sallow face and pale, cold eyes. He wore no hat, and his sand-colored hair matted across his forehead.

"Mornin', Earl!" Benny's voice was falsely hearty. "This here's Rafer . . . he come in jes' a few minutes 'fore you, lookin' for the dispatcher's job."

Earl didn't answer, and Benny's voice trailed weakly away. The straw boss hung his coat on a hook. He wore a gray work shirt that stretched shapelessly across his heavy shoulders and arms and trousers that strained around his hamlike thighs. When he sat down, the desk seemed absurdly small for his bulk.

"I'll bring you coffee, Earl," Benny said. "I jes' made you a fresh pot."

He carried a mug of coffee to Earl at the desk. When the straw boss picked it up, the mug sank in his huge hand.

"Like I was sayin', Earl," Benny began again, "Rafer come

in jes' a few minutes 'fore you." He turned to Rafer for confirmation.

"I just got here," Rafer said.

Earl still hadn't said a word.

"I tol' him if you din' wanna talk now, he gotta come back later." Benny gave Rafer an apologetic look.

When Earl finally spoke, his voice was deep and hoarse.

"Where you from?"

"I ast' 'em that same question 'fore you come in," Benny said quickly. "He tol' me—"

A warning hiss from Earl snapped Benny into silence.

"Where'd you hear about the job?"

"It was posted on the board at the Pacific Garden Mission."

"You a drunk or a junkie?"

"No," Rafer said. The word came tightly from his dry throat.

"Don't lie to me." Earl's eyes held him like teeth.

"I've been a drunk in the past," Rafer said. "But I just finished the sobriety program. I mean to stay dry now."

Earl continued staring at Rafer as if watching for the slightest quiver to betray a lie. Hard as he tried to meet Earl's gaze, Rafer had to look away.

"Ever worked in an office?"

"Last year I dispatched for a taxi company in Detroit. I think I can get you a reference."

"To hell with references," Earl said. "You do your job or you're out."

Rafer nodded.

"You want the job, you be here at six tonight," Earl said brusquely. "You'll work from six until six in the morning."

"That's fine with me," Rafer said, surprised at how quickly Earl had decided to hire him. He started to ask about the pay and then thought it better to wait. Benny could tell him about the wages later.

"I'll show him the ropes, Earl," Benny said.

"Show him the ropes?" Earl's voice dripped with contempt. "A useless shit like you couldn't show him how to spit."

Benny's face went bloodless. He licked his lips and looked wretchedly down at his desk.

"Just give him the phone numbers and tell him who to call." Earl's tone had gone from harsh to mocking. "You got brains enough to do that?"

"Sure, Earl," Benny said weakly.

Earl pointed a big finger at Rafer. "Now you listen to me," he said. "Make sure you get the orders right. You fuck them up and there'll be hell to pay. When the trucks come in, make sure any ice left goes into the big house. And don't get too friendly with the men. I hear one of them say anything good about you, I'll know you're not doing your job. Understand?"

"Yes sir."

"Six sharp," Earl said. "If you're late, don't bother to come at all."

Rafer nodded and picked up his coat and hat. He started to tell Benny good-bye, and then, because the old man was avoiding his gaze, he said nothing.

As Rafer stepped from the office into the cold dawn air, grateful to be out of Earl's presence, he inhaled deeply to relieve the pressure in his chest.

He heard the cooing of the pigeons on the pole, and several took flight into the gray sky. In that first dim light, the Team Track seemed even more desolate than it had appeared in the rain the night before. From the railroad yards below the hill, the banging of the freights and the bells of the engines shattered the cold, damp air.

Rafer tugged up the collar of his coat, dug his hands into his pockets, and started down the hill. Near the bottom, he encountered two shabbily dressed men whose faces he remembered seeing at the mission.

"You guys after the dispatcher's job?" he asked.

The men nodded.

"I'll save you walking up the hill," Rafer said. "The job's filled."

He didn't wait to see if they believed him or not but started down Halsted Street. In the stark dawn, the taverns were locked and dark. He passed a few homeless men sleeping in doorways beneath ragged coats or under layers of newspaper and cardboard.

A few blocks from his hotel, chilled from the long walk, Rafer stopped in an all-night diner for coffee and a roll. Sipping hot coffee, he felt elated because he'd found work. He'd been wise not to wait until morning.

He pulled a small lined notebook from his coat pocket and opened it. He dug for his pencil, and slowly, careful to keep his writing legible, he began a letter to his family.

Dearest Mellie and Rosie:

I came out yesterday after three weeks in the addiction center. I know I have been through these treatments before but this seemed a really good program with caring people. I feel better than I've felt in a long time and I'm vowing, dear Mellie, this time I'm going to make it.

Now for some good news. I just got hired as a dispatcher and I'm starting work tonight! Finding a job so soon after getting out of the program is a good omen. I have a feeling before too long I'll be able to come home!

The weather here is still rainy and cold. I don't mind putting up with it when I think of both of you in the sun. From my first check I'll start saving money for the trip home. I love you both so much,

Rafer

He tore the pages from the notebook and folded them to mail when he got back to the hotel.

He lingered over his coffee, the euphoria he had expressed in the letter slowly fading. He recalled Earl's venomous face and Benny's terror, and a foreboding swept over him. He wondered whether he should bother going back. Then he thought again of Mellie and Rosie and felt an intense longing to hold them both in his arms. Clasping that dream subdued his fears and anxieties about Earl and the job.

3

Mike

MIKE DROVE HIS FIVE-YEAR-OLD CHEVY SOUTH ON Halsted and at Fifteenth Street turned up the gravel road that he had driven thousands of times. The rain that had fallen the night before had left the ruts filled with puddles. As the weather turned colder, the water would freeze, and the trucks would bounce and rock over ridges of ice. When the weather warmed, the ruts would fill with water once more. In the heat of the summers, the roadway grew dry and scorched in the hot sun. The parched ground soaked up the puddles of melting ice, and the truck wheels whipped up spirals of dust that clogged his nostrils and throat.

Mike parked beside the garage and emerged into the shadowed landscape of the Team Track. More than half his life had been spent among these weather-worn buildings. Even in the blackest night, he could describe every part of the location as clearly as if he were seeing it in daylight.

There was the shabby, single-windowed office under the light pole on which pigeons roosted; the garage smelling of gasoline and grease; the big house misted with frozen vapors from the blocks of ice; the locker room smelling of sweat and tobacco, noisy with the laughter and horseplay of drivers and helpers.

Now, it was true that Earl was an inescapable part of this world, as well. As soon as Mike opened the office door, he saw the straw boss looming like a mastodon above his desk. Even in winter, the great layers of his fat exuded a sour odor. Mike pitied the men who worked with him in the office.

Benny sat at his desk beside the new man that Mike had met in the locker room the night before.

"'Lo, Mike," Benny greeted him in a muted voice.

"Hi'ya doing, Benny."

Benny gestured at the new man. "This here's Rafer. He's gonna be workin' here now."

Mike gave no sign that he had met the man before. "Hi'ya, Rafer."

"Glad to meet you, Mike."

In the dim light of the locker room the night before, Mike hadn't noticed the new man's pale cheeks and anxious eyes that were the mark of a boozer. He was surprised that Earl had hired him. But knowing the straw boss's cruelty, Mike thought Earl might have put Rafer on the payroll only so he could torment him.

Mike crossed the office to stand before Earl's desk. The straw boss didn't look up from his papers. Ignoring someone waiting to talk to him was one of the ways Earl made men nervous. Mike wouldn't be drawn into that mean-spirited gambit by saying or doing anything to suggest he was anxious or impatient. He waited calmly until the straw boss was ready to look up.

Earl had been transferred from the company offices downtown to the Team Track as straw boss fifteen years earlier. At the time, it was rumored he had been exiled to that shabby outpost because of problems he had getting along with people.

Even if his disposition hadn't been so venomous, Mike couldn't imagine Earl's bulk and snarl fitting in among normal-sized men and women in any office.

From the beginning, Earl had seen Israel, Pacheco, and Mike as adversaries. They weren't afraid of him, and their refusal to be intimidated weakened his tyranny over the young icemen. After Pacheco died and Israel was forced by his arthritic limbs to retire, Earl focused his hostility on Mike.

Israel condemned Earl as a disciple of Satan. Mike couldn't accept the straw boss as a creature from some demonic domain.

He suspected Earl's malice and enmity came because of his jealousy of Israel and of Mike, and, finally, of all the icemen. They were quick and agile as they worked high on the runways of the railroad cars. Earl was stone-footed and slow, doomed to remain forever rooted to the earth.

There were other contrasts. While Earl kept reminding the men that their labor was menial and humbling, Mike fought to foster pride in them about the work they were doing and the importance of doing their job well. As long as Mike encouraged excellence in the icemen, Earl couldn't really rule them. That fueled his frustration and anger against Mike.

When Earl finally looked up, he spoke with a false, mocking concern in his voice.

"How you feel tonight, Greek?"

"I feel fine!" Mike said. "I feel like an iceman. How do you feel, Earl?"

"You look tired," Earl scowled. "A man shouldn't look as tired as you at the start of his shift."

"Hard workers like you and me can't help getting tired, Earl," Mike said genially. "I guess I just show it while a big-muscled man like you is able to hide it."

Benny sat hunched in his chair with his back to them, his shoulders trembling with the tension of the confrontation. The new man remained bent over his desk.

From the locker room beyond the office came the voices of the icemen who had finished the day shift and were changing to leave. Mendoza would be at the big house, loading their truck.

Earl glared up at Mike, who felt him struggling for some venomous response.

He knew that for years the straw boss had wanted to fire him. But Earl needed an exceptional reason because the yardmasters in all the locations respected Mike and the bosses downtown knew the quality of his work. Earl's only recourse was to assign Mike the most difficult runs and schedule him to work night icing calls, that should have been assigned to men with less seniority, hoping to force him to quit. Mike accepted those pressures

Earl imposed on him and vowed he wouldn't let the straw boss drive him out.

"Why the hell don't you quit like the doctor told you?" Earl said harshly. "I sent his report downtown and I'm expecting to hear from them any day now about letting you go. Why don't you save yourself the fuss and get out now? With all the dough you made, you could buy a bar and hang out with the other old Greeks."

"I'll be honest, Earl, and tell you what stops me," Mike said gravely. "All these years I know you been worrying I might get hurt or sick. Hell, if I left and you didn't have me to fret about, think how unhappy you'd be. That's the reason I'm sticking around."

Benny cleared his throat with a dry croaking sound.

Earl's lips quivered in fury. He threw the job slips across the desk.

"Get the hell out, Greek, and do your work!"

For a raging moment Mike considered the raw joy of pounding his fist into Earl's beefy face. He masked his loathing, picked up the slips, and turned to leave.

"See you later, Benny," he said. He nodded at Rafer and turned to leave the office, feeling Earl's eyes cutting like knives into his back.

Inside the locker room, Sigmund and Thadeus, two of the year-round veterans, were changing at their lockers. Mike greeted them with the few words he knew in Polish, and they nodded silently in response. They were stolid, impassive men, their burly bodies and stoic visages close as twins. Mike had worked with them for twenty years and knew little more about them at the end of that time than he had known in the beginning.

Stamps and Noodles, the other two veterans who made up the year-round crews, had both started at the Team Track in the 1930s and then left to fight in the war. At war's end, after being discharged, both returned to their jobs at the Team Track.

Stamps was a muscular black man, one of the strongest and most skilled of the icemen. He had served as an infantryman in some of the fiercest battles of the war, first in North Africa and then in the Allied invasion of Europe. He rarely spoke of those experiences, but Mike knew they had left him scarred. There were times when Stamps turned silent and morose, withdrawing for hours into his own brooding thoughts.

Noodles, a red-headed, big-boned hillbilly from the Tennessee mountains, with a wide-toothed grin and a cocky demeanor, had been a marine. He had been part of the marine landing force that fought on the bloody island of Iwo Jima.

If the war had left Stamps haunted and somber, it made Noodles flippant and reckless, unwilling to take his work or his life seriously.

"Hey, Mike," Noodles greeted him with a grin. "You look ready to chew on raw meat. You and Elephant Man must have had one of your sweet, friendly talks."

"You got it all wrong, Noodles," Mike said. "The big fellow and me are getting along much better. I think he's even beginning to like me."

"That man doesn't like anybody, even his mama," Noodles scoffed.

"This is no time for you to be coming to work, Mike," Stamps spoke quietly, staring with contempt toward Earl's office. "That pissbully got no right to keep you working nights like this, week after week. Noodles and me can tell him we'll take your shift."

"Don't worry about it, Stamps, and don't ask him to do anything for me," Mike said. "He'd only kick it back in your teeth. I'll be off this shift pretty soon now."

From his locker Mike took a bulky, frayed woolen jacket to replace his good fleece one. He changed his footwear, putting on the steel capped safety shoes to protect his feet from falling ice. As he finished lacing his shoes, he heard the rumble of the HiLift truck outside on the hill. A moment later Mendoza sauntered into the locker room.

"All loaded and ready, Mike," he said. "Where we going first?"

"Proviso, then Seventy-ninth Street. We'll finish up with a potato car in Markham."

"Well, let's roll then!" Mendoza said. "The quicker we start, the sooner we finish!"

"Give those potatoes my best wishes, boys," Noodles waved them good-bye. "Stamps and me are going to have ribs at the Pit. Hey, Mendoza, I'll save you a few bones."

"A dog wouldn't want your bones," Mendoza grinned.

Mike and Mendoza walked outside to the HiLift waiting with its motor idling and blocks wedged beneath its front wheels. Above the Team Track, the stars glittered in a cold, moonless night sky.

Mike swung up into the cab. Mendoza kicked the blocks from under the wheels and joined him. Mike shifted into gear, the motor surging and the wheel vibrating in his hands. The HiLift rocked down the hill.

Mendoza opened the small package of baklava Mike had brought him and ate the pieces with relish, licking his fingers at the end.

"This stuff is so damn good, I'm going to ask my mama to learn to make it."

"You got to be Greek to make good baklava," Mike said. "It's in the blood."

They drove in silence for a while, the only sound in the cab the rumbling of the motor.

"It's still damn cold, but I swear I'm starting to feel spring in my bones," Mendoza said. "This time of year, back in Nogales, all nine of us in my family, we'd be planting and seeding." A wistfulness entered his voice. "Only thing I'm planting now is blocks of ice into bunkers."

"You're saving all those carloads of fruits and vegetables from rotting," Mike said. "That should please your farmer's heart."

In the Proviso yards, they got the location of the cars from the yardmaster. Mike parked the truck alongside the first car, and carrying his tools and a lantern, he rode up on the cage. Mendoza climbed the train ladder and joined him on top of the car.

By lantern light, they opened the bunker plugs. With the narrow beams to guide them, they dragged the blocks from the HiLift cage to the runway. They swiftly cut the blocks into smaller chunks and used their tongs to fling the chunks into the bunkers.

They worked quickly and smoothly on the narrow runway. To save their wind, they didn't speak, but Mendoza hummed a fragment of a song.

When the first pair of bunkers were full, they added rock salt and replaced the plugs. Mendoza walked along the runway while Mike drove the truck to the other end of the car. He joined Mendoza on top of the car once again.

Icing always had to be done carefully, but the labor became more hazardous at night with the runways lit only by lanterns. There was added danger when the particles of ice froze. But Mike had worked on the cars for so long, he knew exactly where to place his feet, how to balance his body, how to swing his arms. He could cut down a four-hundred-pound block in the dark without making a false step or a wasted move.

As he swivelled and rotated his body through the motions of icing, his arms and legs slipped into a seamless rhythm. A surge of blood stoked his muscles, his lungs and heart expanded, his strength multiplied. As he had experienced so many times before, he felt a joy in what he was doing, the reason he was born, the purpose for his life.

When they finished at Proviso, Mike drove along Milwaukee Avenue toward the Santa Fe yards. The headlights of passing cars flashed across the frost-rimmed windshield, and he squinted to see the street. A gust of cold wind carrying a scent of rain seeped in through the loose frame of the cab window. Mendoza shivered beside him.

"If we ever get a damn truck with windows that close and a heater that works," Mendoza said gloomily, "I'll give my paycheck to the church."

"Your church's got a long wait," Mike said.

Inside the Santa Fe yards, they were delayed at a crossing by a passing freight train. They waited while the bells rang and the flashing barrier lights reddened the darkness.

"I was watching you back at Proviso," Mendoza said. "I'm twenty years younger, and I been icing for ten years now. I'm probably even stronger than you too but damn if you still don't ice quicker and better than me . . . hell, not just me . . . better than anyone else at the Team Track."

"You're a good iceman now, Mendoza," Mike said. "When you've iced for as long as I have, you'll be a better iceman yet."

"Wouldn't make a damn difference how long I ice," Mendoza shook his head. "I'd never be near as good. The ice belongs to you. That's just the way it is."

The freight passed and the barriers rose. Mike drove across the tracks.

Mendoza was right in saying the ice belonged to him, but that wasn't the way Mike wanted it. He had tried for years to find someone who might follow in the path that guided his life.

From each batch of new men who came for the summer work, Mike chose the best among them to tutor and guide. He had been hopeful a number of times when a man showed a spark of ability. In the end, none of them had proven to have the devotion that was needed. That was also true of the skillful, good veterans he worked with now.

For Sigmund and Thadeus, older men with only a few years of work left before them, the icing was a job they did without passion or pleasure.

Stamps had the strength and the skill, but the war had left him drained of any pleasure in life or work, his energies consumed by his dark memories.

Noodles, who was also a skillful iceman, was a lighthearted jester who had never shown a fragment of commitment to the ice or to anything else.

The one who showed the most promise was Mendoza. The young man was talented and strong and, at times, seemed to truly enjoy the icing. Mike had worked hard to tutor him, and Mendoza was a bright and apt pupil. For a while, Mike believed he had found his successor. But the obsession that drove Mendoza was gambling and pursuing the girls in the bordellos. These consumed most of his energy and his paycheck except for a sum he sent home each week to his family in Mexico.

Now it was true that Mike spent time in the bordello as well.

For the last few years, he'd even had a special woman, Dolores, that he visited weekly. But that relationship never overshadowed the work he did on the truck. Each of his lives had its place without infringing on the other.

Their final stop was to ice a potato car at Markham. As they were finishing, the yardmaster brought them a message from Benny with an order for the I.C.—the Illinois Central railroad—in Blue Island. They made that assignment, as well, and then drove back to the Team Track.

Mike hadn't been aware of aches or soreness while he worked. Now, gripping the jolting wheel of the truck, pain curled from his back into his shoulders and he felt haplessly drained of strength.

He looked a little enviously at the young iceman beside him. Mendoza didn't seem at all tired, humming cheerfully under his breath.

"You said you been at the Team Track ten years now," Mike said.

"Starting my eleventh year this June."

"You planning to stick around?"

"This coming year could be my last," Mendoza said. "I been writing letters to a girl back home. She's working, saving her money, thinking, someday, we're going to be married."

"Is that what you're thinking ?"

"Hell, I don't know, Mike," Mendoza shrugged. "When I'm down home visiting, I love her a lot. When I come back up here, all I can think about are the girls at the Pink Garden. I like that one week I can lay down with a golden-haired beauty and the next week with a dark-haired sweetheart. I tell you, Mike, I love to look at the whores and touch them and smell them! I don't know how I'd feel if I had to love the same woman week after week."

"Don't marry that girl back home until you're damn sure you're ready to settle down!" Mike said fiercely. "Don't make her your wife unless you can be faithful. You hear me?"

"I hear you—" Mendoza seemed startled at Mike's outburst. "Maybe I just got to get other women out of my system first." He looked at Mike. "Didn't you tell me once that you'd been married?"

"I was once," Mike said. "We got divorced."

"I'm sorry, Mike," Mendoza said quietly. "I shouldn't have brought it up."

"That's all right," Mike said. "It was a long time ago."

At Fifteenth Street, Mike turned the truck off Halsted and started up the hill.

"Hop off at the lockers if you want," Mendoza said. "I'll unload the ice that's left."

"You loaded the truck by yourself last night," Mike said gruffly. "You think I can't do my share?"

"Let's face it, Mike," Mendoza grinned, "You're getting a little long in the tooth, and you're slowing down too. It's only right a strong young buck like me helps out an old fart."

"Mendoza, you got a big heart," Mike said. He reached over casually and brought his bunched fist down hard on Mendoza's leg above the knee. Mendoza bellowed a cry of pain that drowned the noise of the motor.

"That'll teach you a little respect for this old fart."

Mendoza rubbed his leg and groaned.

"Daddy," he said. "When I grow up, daddy, can I be a Greek iceman like you?"

"You could become the greatest damn iceman in the world!" Mike cried, "but you'll never be Greek!"

They laughed and Mike braked the truck to a stop before the big house platform. He and Mendoza transferred the remaining ice into the big house. Mike slammed the heavy freezer door.

"I'll park the rig and meet you at the lockers," he said.

Mendoza started limping down the hill, still rubbing his leg.

"You damn near crippled me!" he called back. "I may never be able to work a HiLift again." He waved Mike an obscene gesture of farewell.

Mike parked the HiLift beside the row of trucks and switched off the motor. Weariness made him unwilling to move, and he leaned back with a sigh against the seat of the cab.

He hadn't told Mendoza the full truth about his marriage. His wife, Natalie, had left him some years before they divorced and taken his son, Lucas, who'd been five then, with her.

Mike spent the first months after their departure frantically phoning and writing Natalie's relatives and various friends. Although his efforts proved useless, he continued to believe that she'd change her mind and come back. He also hoped that as the boy became a little older, his son might want to see his father. But the years passed and that reunion never came true.

About five years after Natalie had left, Mike had been served with papers from her lawyer seeking a divorce. He refused to sign them unless he were granted the right to see his son. Her lawyer told him Natalie refused that request but promised that two years later, when the boy was twelve, she'd let him decide whether he wished to see his father.

Mike had no choice but to agree to that provision, and he signed the divorce papers. The year his son became twelve, he waited week after week, month after month, to hear from him. But that year passed and the next few years passed, as well, and he heard nothing.

As the years went by, he came to accept his responsibility for the end of their marriage. He had failed to understand the fidelity his marriage vows required. He loved his wife and son, but he had been unwilling to give up drinking with his cronies and sharing the beds of other women. He'd made endless promises to his wife that he always broke. Then, it was too late.

While he had come to accept the justice of his wife's leaving him, he had never gotten over the loss of his son. Despite all Mike's failures and flaws, that seemed an excessive price to pay. Denying a man his son took away the best of his past and any hope for his future, as well.

He considered it strange how each time he recalled his wife and son, certain images stood out. When he thought of Natalie, he didn't picture her pretty face or her slender figure but the strawberry birthmark on her shoulder and the tortoise shell combs she wore in her long auburn hair.

The image he retained of his son was the boy sitting on the

front steps of their house waiting for him to come home from work. When Mike's car pulled up before the house, the boy would come running and jump into his arms.

In that melancholy moment, through the truck window, a streak of light ripped the blackness of the sky with a radiance that stretched from heaven to earth. After it was gone, a stunning crimson glow lingered in its wake.

When he'd seen shooting stars as a boy in Crete, Mike had wished for a life of high adventure, wealth, and fame. Now, his wish was a simple, fervent one, that before he died he'd be able to embrace the son he had lost.

The hope that his starlit wish might be granted someday lightened his melancholy. He swung out of the cab, and despite his weariness, he walked buoyantly down the hill.

4

Earl

IF THE HOUSE WAS SILENT WHEN EARL ENTERED, the air musty and dry, most likely Nora would be sick and in bed. If there were smells of food from the kitchen or a radio playing, then at least for that night, they'd sit down to dinner as a family.

He always braced himself for the worst, but the silence that night as he opened the door bit like teeth at his flesh. He walked like a mourner down the hallway, past the dark kitchen, to the bedroom where Matthew, his son of ten, and, Julie, his daughter, two years younger, would have taken refuge. The children were sitting on the floor, a board game between them. When she saw him, Julie rose quickly and came to tightly grasp his leg. Matthew didn't move, just kept staring at his father, his eyes large and dark above the pale circles of his cheeks.

"Mama is sick again," Julie said.

Earl stroked his daughter's hair.

"I'll go see her," he said, "and then I'll fix us something to eat."

He left the children's room and walked toward his wife's bedroom. He entered the familiar stench of medications and stale tobacco smoke. Nora lay sprawled across the bed on her belly, dark tentacles of her hair spread across the pillow. Her soiled cotton nightgown wrinkled around her naked thighs, and the soles of her feet were dirty. One hand was concealed beneath her body, and the other, fingers stained and yellow from cigarettes, hung limply over the edge of the bed.

As his shadow loomed across the bed, Nora twisted her head to look up. He saw her drowsy, bloodshot eye.

"How you feeling, hon?" he asked gently.

She uttered a low, hoarse sigh.

"You just take it easy now," he said. "I'll fix the kids something to eat."

"Want water," she slurred the words.

"Sure, hon."

He walked to the kitchen and poured a glass of cold water from the container in the refrigerator and carried it to the bedroom. He tried to help Nora as she struggled to raise her head.

"Too warm."

"It's cold water, hon," Earl said. "I got it right from the refrigerator."

"Too warm!" she said harshly.

Back in the kitchen, he added ice cubes to the water then returned to the bedroom. Nora waved him away.

He placed the glass on the end table.

"When I get some food ready, would you like to eat a little?"

For several minutes he stood helplessly beside the bed.

"You need anything else, hon?"

When she still didn't answer, he turned and left the room.

He heated noodles left over from dinner the night before and boiled a half dozen frankfurters. From the kitchen window he saw lights gleaming in the windows of kitchens across the alley. He envied other families gathering for dinner around their tables, laughing and talking, sharing the events of the day. He contrasted that with the grim silence that hung over their house.

Julie came into the kitchen and began setting the table.

"Shall I put a plate on for mama?"

"She's not hungry right now," Earl said. "I'll take her something to eat later."

He put the food on the table and sat down with the children.

He would have preferred to eat in silence, but he felt compelled to break the sadness of their mood.

"What time did Mrs. Alvin bring you home from school?"

"About four o'clock," Matthew said. "When we got home, Mama was sick again."

Earl had suspected Nora was going to be sick when he left her that morning. They slept in separate, adjoining bedrooms, but to prevent her locking the door between their rooms, he had taken the door down. When she heard him getting up at dawn that morning, she rose, as well. She pulled on a robe and ran her hairbrush several times through the dark tangle of her hair. She insisted she'd make breakfast for the children and started downstairs. Later, when he walked into the kitchen, he found her slumped on a chair in a corner, holding a cigarette and drinking black coffee.

"Give me a minute," she said.

"That's all right, hon," he said. "I'll make breakfast."

"I don't want anything," she said. "Get something for the kids."

The children came into the kitchen and Julie went to hug her mother. Nora whispered something to her. Once they sat down at the table, Julie stared sadly at her mother, while Matthew avoided looking at her.

Earl prepared cereal and eggs, but neither child ate more than a bite. He knew the tension and despair in the house robbed them of any appetite. He was affected, as well, finding it hard to swallow any food. The air in the kitchen was heavy and stifling, making it hard to breath.

After the children got up from the table, Julie kissed her mother good-bye. "Be a good girl," her mother said in a low, weary voice. She fumbled to push aside a strand of Julie's hair that had fallen loose across her cheek.

The children walked outside to wait for the neighbor who would look after them until it was time to drive them to school.

"How about an egg and toast now, hon?" Earl asked. "You'll feel better if you eat something."

"I'm not hungry."

"I'll make you a sandwich in case you get hungry later on," Earl said. "Maybe you'll feel better if you get dressed. Do you want me to help you?"

She didn't answer but fumbled at the pack of cigarettes in the pocket of her robe. He struck a match for her and at the same time contrived to slip the pack from the table into his pocket. He busied himself around the kitchen, delaying his leaving until she had finished the cigarette, fearful that she'd set the house on fire.

"Anything I can get you before I leave, hon?"

Once again she didn't answer, her fingers groping in the pocket of her robe, searching for the cigarette packet he had taken.

Earl bent to give her a kiss. She grimaced as his lips brushed her forehead.

That evening, eating with the children, he noticed with a heavy heart how everything around them bore the signs of disrepair and neglect. The dishes they ate on were chipped, the pans coated with grease that could no longer be scoured away. The paint on the cabinets above the sink was peeling, and the flowered wallpaper, a bright yellow when it was new, was now faded, several corners torn away from the wall.

After they'd finished eating, Julie and Matthew carried their dishes to the sink.

"You both go do your homework now," Earl said. "I'll tell you when it's time for bed."

Julie paused in the doorway.

"Can I say good-night to Mommy before I go to bed?"

"If she's sleeping, you better not bother her. When she wakes up I'll tell her you said good-night."

He pitied the children because their life was so wretched. For every day that Nora felt well, there were four, five days when she was sick. At those times, the children would become tense and silent and retreat to their room.

As he washed the dishes, Earl recalled the early years of their marriage. He often reached back for those memories because the first few years following his marriage were the only time in his life he had been truly happy.

Even as a youth he had been cursed by being oversized and clumsy. Girls laughed at him and boys made him the butt of their jokes. All through high school he was a loner, an outcast. His isolation fostered his meanness and sparked his anger, and he gained a reputation as a brawler. He attacked other youths with a fury that frightened them because they knew that in his rage he was capable of murder. He was also a poor student and nearly flunked out of school several times.

He knew his life would have been different if he had been normal in size. His weight and build were not his fault but caused by something in his heredity. Although his parents, who had died when he was a child, had been normal sized, he had heard that an uncle he had never seen was grossly obese.

Earl tried to exercise and diet and only grew bigger and heavier. But it wasn't merely that he became more obese, it was the bizarre way the fat formed appendages on his body. Fat coiled around his neck, bulged on his upper arms, spread along his thighs. The bigger and more shapeless he became, the more he repulsed himself. He undressed in the dark so he would not have to see his misshapen body.

Then, in his senior year in high school, Nora transferred into his class from another school. She was dark-haired and slender, as pretty as any of the cheerleaders. To prevent himself from being hurt or humiliated, Earl had struck a surliness and indifference toward girls. Nora seemed to understand his vulnerability and worked hard to reassure him. She was the only girl or boy Earl had ever known who seemed to recognize the trembling, longing heart beneath his gargantuan bulk. He marveled at how tender and caring she could be. They studied together, and with her help, he managed to avoid flunking out of school. For a long while, he thought of her as a dear friend, never daring to think it could be anything more.

After they graduated, they continued to see one another. As if he were watching the unfolding of a miracle, he felt her growing love. Her love gave him confidence, and for the first time in his life, he felt a sexual vitality, was able to conceive of himself as lover.

Even in his wildest imaginings, he found it impossible to believe that a nymph so delicate and beautiful could love a grotesque creature like him. In spite of this conviction, somehow, he mustered the courage to ask her to marry him.

To his utter astonishment, she accepted his proposal. When he left her that evening, his joy made him made him feel light-footed for the first time in his life.

They were married in a small neighborhood church in the fall of the year. After his parents died, he had been raised in a foster home by people who'd gotten rid of him as soon as he'd come of age, so he had no family at the wedding. But Nora's parents and her brother were there. He ignored their revulsion at his gross size. He was too immersed in his own good fortune.

On their wedding night, after Nora and he had made love and she'd fallen asleep, his excitement and joy kept him awake. He could not give up feasting on the memory of her beauty, the supple slopes and curves of her body, her breasts and thighs so perfectly formed. When he recalled her naked legs straddling his huge carcass, her dark hair cascading across her shoulders, and, miracle of miracles, love for him in her face, he was so grateful that he wanted to cry out his wonder and joy. He felt as if he were a monster who for the first time had been caressed instead of cursed.

In the beginning of the fourth year of their marriage, Nora became pregnant. From the beginning, her pregnancy was severe and disabling. She was sick most of the nine months, the house assailed by the sound and stink of vomit. She also suffered debilitating headaches and at night endured disruptive dreams that caused her to whimper and moan.

During the day, she remained nervous and distracted, as if she were still battling the unsettling images of her dreams. Despite Earl's desire to help her, there was little he could do and she suffered alone.

Her painful, oppressive pregnancy prompted his fear that they'd have a flawed, misshapen child, a miniature version of his ugliness. But when their son was born, wiping away the traces of Nora's months of suffering, Earl was overjoyed that the baby had all of his mother's beauty and none of his deformity.

Although Nora no longer suffered from daily sickness, her headaches and anxiety continued. Earl took her to a doctor who didn't find any physical problems and put her on a regimen of vitamins and medication. For a couple of weeks, she seemed better, and then the headaches returned. At times they became so severe she couldn't muster the will or strength to get out of bed. Somehow, with Earl's help, they managed to look after the baby son they had named Matthew.

A little more than a year after Matthew was born, Nora became pregnant again. The same pattern of daily sickness that had marked her earlier pregnancy resumed. After their daughter, named Julie for Nora's mother, was born, the relentless headaches that had so disrupted Nora's life returned vengefully. At night, her fitful dreams evolved into nightmares. Instead of moaning and whimpering, she woke screaming. Earl would sit up with her because she had trouble getting back to sleep. After she finally slept, he lay sleepless, waiting tensely for her to scream again. When dawn came, he dragged himself wearily from bed to dress and go to work.

On those days Nora felt well, she was a loving and attentive mother. Her better spirits sparked a lighter mood in the children. Julie was especially sensitive to her mother's feelings and became animated when Nora felt better. At those times her mother was ill, the child grew silent and anxious too.

Nora's depression and anxiety carried from the night into her days. She remained in bed or sat in an armchair in a shadowed corner of her bedroom. She gave up caring how she looked or what she wore, sometimes spending the entire day in her nightgown or wearing a tattered cotton robe. With the aid of caring neighbors, the children were looked after until Earl got home. Then he fed them, bathed them, and put them to bed.

They lived in that condition of tension and anxiety, and Nora continued to grow worse. The demons of her headaches and nightmares became more severe, and a specialist who examined her urged that Earl sign her into the psychiatric ward of a hospital for testing.

Desperate to have her get better, Earl took her to the hospital and had her admitted. He regretted his decision when he went to visit her a day later because he couldn't believe she belonged among the dull, unmoored human wrecks in the ward. The psychiatrists diagnosed schizophrenia, a malady she had lived with for so long they felt it would be almost impossible to help her.

Earl had to look the word up in the dictionary. He kept reading the definition, repeating the words numbly until he knew them by heart. A dozen times a day, they'd come knifing into his head. *A severe mental disorder characterized by disintegration of the process of thinking and contact with reality. Hallucinations and a loss of personal identity are common.*

The doctors recommended Earl commit Nora to an institution for at least a year to undergo treatment, which would include shock therapy.

"Instead of telling me to lock her up, why in hell can't you do something to help her?" Earl stormed at the doctors. "Can't you find some new medicine, some new treatment! Every day you read about miracle pills curing all kinds of sickness! A goddam fool don't need a medical degree to say, 'lock her up!' Why the hell can't you help her?"

His size and his anger frightened them, and they tried to avoid him. His repeated calls to their offices went unanswered.

Earl tried to convince himself that Nora might be better looked after and helped if she were in an institution. But when he thought of her in the hands of uncaring strangers, strapped and bound to a bed or chair, her flesh pricked with needles shooting drugs into her to keep her quiet, he felt the sting of tears and rage.

Whatever agony her illness forced upon her, he couldn't let her endure alone. As she had cared for and loved him in his time of need, he had to provide her a loving, caring heart in her own travails.

In Nora's calmer, more lucid moments, she seemed to understand the anguish her sickness was causing her family.

"It would be better for all of you if I died," she said quietly. "Then you and the kids could be rid of me. That's the only way you'll ever find peace."

"Don't say that, Nora," Earl pleaded. "You'll get better, you'll see. Don't give up hope."

"I won't get better," she spoke in a low, dreary voice. "I'll be sick and crazy until the day I die. There will be no end to it. And, God help me, for all our sakes, I want to die."

He couldn't bear to see her eyes well up with tears. Even as he cried himself, he vowed to look after her and protect her.

Once, when Nora had been feeling better for almost a week, in a fit of euphoria, Earl took her and the children to a neighborhood Chinese restaurant. They hadn't eaten out in almost a year and the children were excited at that rare outing, even the normally somber Matthew smiling. They entered the restaurant in a buoyant mood, sitting among other families at the adjoining tables. Earl was so gratified at Nora's good mood and the children's happiness that he ignored the stares and furtive whispers of other patrons about his size.

They studied the menus and ordered their dinner. Nora sat smiling faintly, looking lovelier than she had in a long time. Thrilled at the prospect of going out, she had tried on several dresses, asking Earl how she looked in each one. He assured her she looked wonderful in all of them. When she finally chose a light, flowered frock, he told her she had made the right choice.

The waiter brought the platters of steaming food to their table. He placed Nora's shrimp-and-noodle casserole down before her and lifted the lid. Nora stared at the hot food emitting curls of steam with a sudden, unsettling intensity.

Earl understood some alteration in Nora's mercurial mind was taking place. He watched her warily as he served Julie from another platter. Nora made no move to eat, her eyes fixated on the food, her jaw trembling as if she were trying to bite her lower lip.

Earl moved his chair closer to her and served some of the shrimp and noodles from the casserole onto her plate.

"This sure looks delicious, hon," he said. "I'll try one and tell you how good it tastes."

Whether it was the food or his own terror at what he feared might happen, the shrimp tasted like a rubbery mass and he almost gagged.

"I don't want it," Nora said.

"It tastes great, hon," Earl said. "You always liked shrimp and noodles."

"I don't want it!" She raised her voice, and the other patrons stared at them. Julie and Matthew had stopped eating and were watching their mother. "Take it away!"

"All right, hon," Earl said soothingly. "Would you like something else? I'll call the waiter and get you something else."

Then, before he could take the food away from her, with a shrill, explosive scream, Nora swept the plate from the table. It landed with a deafening clatter on the floor, the plate shattering, the shrimp and noodles strewn around the feet of the people at the surrounding tables.

Nora screamed again, the piercing sound echoing through the restaurant, shocking and freezing people at their tables.

Earl kicked back his chair and lurched to his feet. He put his hands around Nora's shoulders, trying desperately to calm her. As she continued to fight him, he managed to tug her to her feet and started pulling her to the door. All the time she kept screaming.

The children hobbled along behind them, Matthew pale with terror and Julie crying.

"Watch out for your sister!" Earl cried to his son.

As they struggled and stumbled from the dining room to the door, the agitated proprietor pursued them, waving the check and shrieking at them in Chinese.

"I'll be back, goddam you!" Earl shouted. "Can't you see she's sick! You'll get your goddam money!"

As he half-carried Nora past the cashier, several people entering the restaurant quickly got out of his way. He saw their shocked, pitying faces.

"What in hell you looking at?" he bellowed. "You never seen a woman get sick before! You goddam buzzards!"

When he finally got Nora out of the restaurant and into the parking lot, just as suddenly as she had erupted, her mood altered once again and she grew quiet. She ceased fighting and let him help her into the car. She huddled in the back seat, her breathing heavy and weary, as if the outburst had exhausted her.

Matthew wouldn't ride in the back seat with his mother and Earl let him sit in front. When he pushed his own bulky body into the seat, Matthew was jammed against the door. All the way home, Earl could feel the boy's body trembling. In the back seat, his daughter kept crying in a low, shaken voice.

"It's all right, sweetheart," Earl said. "It's all right now. Mama just got sick. It's not her fault. We'll be home soon."

The experience had torn him up, as well. He felt a loud pounding in his ears, a hollow, hard sound as if something had exploded in his head. His chest felt constricted, making it difficult for him to breath without pain.

In that terrible moment, he understood the doctors were right. His wife would remain sick and mad for as long as she lived.

Nora's lucid moments became fewer. She had searing headaches during the day, nightmares at night, and her mood swings grew more violent. Earl tried to help her get ready for bed at night, and she unleashed a torrent of abuse against him. As if to make up for those few years of caresses and affection, her fury was boundless. The focus of her wrath was his bulk.

"You aren't human," she said in a low, hoarse voice. "Look at you! You're an elephant, only uglier. You're disgusting to look at, the rolls of fat, your fat, shapeless, stupid face! You turn my stomach!"

He tried not to listen to her tirades. Slowly, laboriously, he'd get her undressed. Seeing her naked, he grieved at the ravages that sickness and neglect of her body had caused. Her skin, once so pale and smooth, had become coarse and dull. Her breasts had a mushroom's mottled coldness, her nipples withered like the pits of small dark olives. She fought him each time he tried to wash her hair and it stuck together in soiled and greasy strands.

He'd bring a wet wash cloth and struggle to wipe her face and hands. She fought him, cursed and spit at him. When exhaustion finally quieted her, her terror of the nightmares sleep brought was the only time she welcomed his touch. She fumbled for his hand and gripped it so hard that her nails cut into his flesh.

He'd hold her small hand enclosed in his huge palm. In those hours he sat beside her, he came to know her hand as if it were part of his own body—dryness of the skin, the ridges of her knuckles, the tremors in her palm, her fingertips cold as the fingers of someone dead.

He also became familiar with the sounds of night. Within the house, he heard water dripping in the bathroom washbasin, the creaking of floorboards, the ticking of a clock. From the street, a car door slammed, a dog barked, drunken voices rose from the pavement below their windows, in the distance a siren wailed. In those moments when all other sounds were stilled, he could hear the slow, labored beating of his heart deep in the cavern of his chest.

If Nora's nightmares did not wake him again, he sometimes fell asleep in the chair and opened his eyes to faint, gray daylight. He'd be stiff and cramped, Nora's hand still enclosed in his own.

After a few such nights, he'd suffer the stupidity of sleeplessness. During the day at work he lost his thought in the middle of a sentence, stumbled over words, forgot the names of men he had worked with for years.

In an effort to get some rest, he'd arrange for caretakers to come in and look after his wife during the day and to sit with her at night. After a few days, Nora's curses and abuse would drive them away. Yet she kept the brunt of her fury for him, condemning his bulk, his stupidity, his sexual deficiencies.

"Can you even see your prick?" she taunted him. "Does it even

Current Check-Outs summary for STANTON,
Sat Sep 13 13:20:05 CDT 2008

BARCODE: 31539002164663
TITLE: The strange case of Dr. Jekyll an
DUE DATE: Sep 27 2008

BARCODE: 31539002006336
TITLE: Twilight of the ice / Harry Mark
DUE DATE: Sep 27 2008

exist anymore or are you pissing from a hole like a woman? You're not a man, you're a mass of blubber, a pair of eyes, a nose and a mouth, emerging from the carcass of a whale! Tub of lard! Barrel of grease! You're a goddam freak who belongs in a circus freak show!"

He was tormented by the abuse that came from her lips. He knew all the obscenities, but the words she hurled tore at his spirit.

Despite the ferocity of her attack, he could never shout back at her in anger, could never raise one of his hamlike fists to threaten or strike her. He understood she was ill and not responsible for the rage that stormed from her disrupted brain. But he was also helpless to respond to her tirades because he loved her. He loved her and remembered with an ache in his heart how she had once loved him.

The only redemption in their wretched lives were the children, comely and quiet, their faces revealing bewilderment at what was happening to their mother. What kept him from going mad himself was his terror at what might happen to them if he were lost, as well. He could not bear the thought of their being parentless, shunted from foster home to foster home where they would be unloved, if not abused.

For the first time, a terrible thought possessed him, that he should kill his wife and children and then himself. The compulsion persisted so deeply in his thoughts that he bought a gun he hid behind the furnace in the cellar.

The thought of murdering his family would come to him when he cut a piece of meat at dinner, while he put the children to bed, during those sleepless hours when he sat beside Nora, the instant he opened his eyes in the morning. He began to believe that it was the only way to spare his family and himself further suffering. Meanwhile, the bile and bitterness festered within him. He felt himself the most cursed creature in the world, condemned to a life of wretchedness and despair. He tried to pray, but he had been so long without any religion that God denied him now. He wondered what he and Nora had done to deserve so dreadful a fate.

He knew only the Team Track saved him from murder. If he hadn't had that desolate, godforsaken outpost to vent his bitterness and rage, he might indeed have been driven to kill his family.

In the years before the Team Track, he had worked in the South Side steel mills and then as a loader on the railway express. After a year, he became a foreman. When the railway depot was closed, he found work as parts manager of a small auto repair shop.

Wherever he worked, he quickly became the butt of jokes and whispers. He discovered that men and women were equally cruel and intolerant of anyone who stood out because of some abnormality. They might have been less cruel and more tolerant if he had been crippled or blind, impediments over which he had no control. But in some perverse way, they branded him responsible for his outlandish size. He could sense the mockery and derision whenever he entered a room, although no one ever dared say anything to his face.

After he and Nora married, her brother, who was a manager with the Crystal Ice Company in Chicago, got Earl a job. He began in accounting, handling bills of lading, a position that required him to make trips into the office where the white collar employees worked. A dozen times a day, he had to run the gauntlet of all the normal-sized, neatly-dressed men and women at their desks who regarded him as a monstrosity. He knew they laughed at him behind his back, mocking his obesity, his inability to sit in a chair without overflowing the seat, how he always wore loafers because he couldn't bend to tie the laces on his shoes. There was even graffiti about him on the bathroom walls, lewd drawings showing him in the act of sex with an elephant. He hadn't committed any crime, but they hounded him as though he were a criminal. He hadn't been guilty of any theft or lie, yet they treated him as though he were a liar and a thief. His rage nurtured his hate for everything and everyone.

When Nora's brother retired from the ice company, Earl feared he'd be fired. Instead, he was transferred from the company's headquarters office to manage icing operations at a South

Side location called the Team Track. He was so grateful for that reprieve that when he was told, he almost broke down and wept. For the first time in his life, that rough, coarse world was where he felt he belonged.

From the beginning, afraid of being fired, he drove the workers at the Team Track mercilessly. The operation had been run carelessly, with bills of lading lost or misplaced too often. In addition, thousands of pounds of ice were allowed to melt overnight on the trucks.

Within a few months, by introducing a stringent discipline and eliminating waste, Earl had made the operation profitable. One of the principal reasons the Team Track began to save on costs was that Earl was obsessive about the unused blocks of ice being taken off the trucks and stored back in the big house.

He began his rule at the Team Track with the desire to stem the losses and make the location profitable. But as his power grew and he saw how men feared him, he used the Team Track as a release for the helplessness and frustration he felt at home. For the first time in his life, instead of being a victim and butt of scorn, he had the power to make others suffer.

Yet even as he ruthlessly ruled the Team Track, he couldn't blind himself to the fact that he worked among better men than he was. He could only conceal his mediocrity before men like Israel, Pacheco, and Mike Zervakis by being brutal to them. With Pacheco dead and Israel gone from the HiLifts, only Mike remained to remind Earl of his failings.

Earl had moments when he wanted to extend his hand to Mike, call him friend, confess his admiration. To Earl who was cursed with clumsiness and gracelessness, the iceman seemed a matchless athlete, making the ice and the trucks an extension of his strength and extraordinary skill. But Earl had Nora and his children to care for, and he dared not allow anyone, even Mike, recognize him as vulnerable and weak.

So his agony continued. He had no friend in whom to confide, no one to help lighten his burden by listening to his grievance. Thinking about Nora and his children and the utter hopelessness of their future, he felt a turmoil in his chest, his heart flailing wildly like the struggle of a dog struck by a car.

In the end, he saw his family and himself, and the iceman Mike Zervakis, as if they were players in a drama, each of them assigned a role, with only God or the devil able to foretell how the monstrous play might end.

5

Rafer

WITH HIS FIRST PAYCHECK, RAFER BOUGHT SEVeral shirts and a pair of pants he sorely needed from a Maxwell Street stall. At the end of his first month of work, he also purchased a twelve-year-old Ford from Noodles for fifteen dollars. The car's fenders were rusted and the interior dilapidated, its wheels rattled, and its ancient motor sputtered. Salvatore, the Team Track mechanic, patched and tuned up the car for him.

"Let me put it this way, Rafer," Salvatore, stocky-bodied with black glossy hair, said. "Use these wheels only to drive back and forth to work, the wreck might hold together a while. Drive it any further, the rattletrap will fall apart under you."

Noodles, standing nearby, protested vehemently.

"That's a hell of a good car!" Noodles said indignantly. "I drove it all over the country! All it needs is a better mechanic than you to get it ship-shape!"

"Sure, sure, Noodles, this wreck is a good car," Salvatore scoffed. "And so's could I whip Joe Louis with one hand tied behind me."

However poor its condition, the car provided Rafer transportation to and from work. He also moved from his cramped cubicle in the Poinsettia to a small, private room and shared a bathroom with one other man instead of having to share a communal shower. For the first time in months, Rafer felt a sense of well-being that came with having a car and a few dollars in his pocket. In addition, every week that he managed to avoid taking a drink buoyed his confidence. He allowed himself to hope he might be on the way to beating his demon.

At the beginning of May, the weather turned warmer. The last patches of dark ice melted, and the first frail, green buds appeared on the ragged bushes in the vacant lots. One morning, Rafer saw a robin perched on the ledge of his window, and it recalled for him the birds in the springs of his childhood.

The start of May also brought to the Team Track a motley band of young men seeking work. There were laborers from the western railroad track gangs who rode the freights into Chicago and farm boys driving up from the south in battered pickup trucks. Most had come of age since the end of the war and felt cheated of the excitement of combat. They were eager for the summer pay and easy access to women and liquor they missed while working on the railroads or on the isolated farms.

Within the span of several weeks, the locker room was filled with the noisy banter of nearly forty newly hired men. A few had worked the ice trucks during previous summers, but most were novices.

Rafer's days in the office with Earl were tense and stressful. Hard as he tried to avoid the wrath of the straw boss, in his first weeks of work, he received several tongue-lashings from Earl for errors he made.

But none of the tirades he endured equaled Earl's mistreatment of Benny. The old dispatcher came in at five in the evening to work the night shift, and the wretched hour he spent with Earl before the straw boss left earned him a full day's worth of abuse.

"How many years you been working here, you stupid sonofabitch!" Earl cried at Benny one evening. "Isn't it time you got those tracking slips right?"

"I'm sorry, Earl . . ." Benny, pale-faced, his voice trembling, said. "I jes' got mixed up . . ."

"I jes' got mixed up! I jes' got mixed up!" Earl mimicked

Benny's lament. "You been mixed up since the goddam day you were born!"

His own fear of the straw boss and of losing the job he so desperately needed kept Rafer from protesting Earl's cruelty. Afterwards, seeing Benny humiliated and wretched, he felt pity for the old man and a growing hatred for Earl.

The straw boss was also a menacing figure to the new workers, his snarl assaulting their vitality and good spirits. When his mammoth figure loomed in the doorway of the locker room (Rafer heard one of the men refer to Earl as "King Kong"), there was a faltering of voices and a muting of laughter.

"You're not getting paid to loaf in here!" was one of Earl's common harangues. "Get the hell out and load up and be goddam sure you don't leave ice melting overnight on the trucks!"

Each of the veteran icemen became a mentor to the newcomers.

Thadeus and Sigmund, limited by their inability to speak English, used gestures to convey the importance of keeping the iceman's pike pole, tongs, and the three-pronged implement called a devil's fork sharp and clean.

Stamps was a gruff, serious teacher, intolerant of inattention or indifference.

"You listen to me now and you listen damn good!" Stamps spoke sternly to a group of new men. "You think a little crack in a block of ice may not seem important, but a crack can split the block. A hundred-pound chunk lands on your leg or foot, you'll never strut on a dance floor again."

Mendoza and Noodles worked as a team in their mentoring, often using caustic humor to warn about carelessness. "Easiest way in the world for a guy to lose a foot is getting it caught under a bunker lid," Noodles said to a dozen men gathered around. He gestured at Mendoza standing nearby. "You remember Kovacik?"

"How can I ever forget that poor soul," Mendoza said gravely.

"He was a good iceman worked here years ago," Noodles said, "but that fool just wouldn't wear his steel-tipped safety shoes. Mendoza and me warned him and warned him."

"Raised hell with him about it a half dozen times," Mendoza agreed.

"He'd put on his safety shoes in the locker room, all right," Noodles said, "soon as he drove into the yards, he changed to sneakers. One night at Proviso, icing a potato car, a bunker lid slammed down, caught his foot!" Noodles slammed one fist into his other palm. "Damn lid sheared off his toes." He fell silent and stared somberly at the men.

"How many toes did he lose, Noodles?" one man asked.

"Not one toe, or two, or even three," Mendoza picked up the story, his voice low and sad. "That poor devil had every last one of his little pinkies lopped off."

"Surgeon couldn't have done a better job!" Noodles said. "One minute Kovacik had a foot like you and me! Then all he had was a bloody stump!"

The men's faces revealed sympathy and distress.

"A hell of a thing to happen," one man muttered. Several others nodded in agreement.

"Remember what the poor bastard did then?" Noodles asked Mendoza.

"How could I ever forget," Mendoza said dolefully.

"Kovacik went into the hospital," Noodles continued slowly, "and he had the doctor cut all the toes off his other foot!"

The men stared at Noodles in bewildered silence.

"Why the hell would he do that?" a shocked young man asked.

"Kovacik felt it was the only way," Mendoza said nodding sagely. "Noodles will tell you why."

Every man in the group looked back at Noodles, waiting tensely for him to explain.

"Kovacik was a good iceman," Noodles said, "but he was also one cheap iceman. After he lost his toes, every time he needed new shoes, he had to buy two pairs, one to fit one foot and one to fit the other. By cutting off the toes on his other foot, he only had to buy one pair!"

Unable to restrain his gloomy demeanor any longer, Mendoza burst into laughter. Noodles joined him, his face contorted with delight. A few men looked sheepish at having been duped, while others turned away in disgust.

Despite all the warnings about safety, there were still accidents. Most were minor cases of sprained muscles or bruises. There were a few more serious mishaps when men slipped off the wet roofs of railroad cars. Several men suffered broken arms and one a broken leg. A farmer broke his collarbone.

Rafer also witnessed what could have been a serious accident when a worker was fastening tail chains on the rear of a truck. The driver in the cab turned on the motor and put the truck in reverse. As the truck lurched backward, Mike, who was standing nearby jerked the worker aside just in time to prevent him being crushed against the garage wall.

Mike stormed around the truck to the cab.

"I'm sorry, Mike!" the driver stammered. "I didn't see him!"

"You melon-headed boob!" Mike cried. "You didn't see him because you didn't look around! Don't back up the damn truck until you're sure its clear behind you!"

Another time Rafer saw Mike lose his temper came when he witnessed several men stabbing playfully at one another with their pike poles. Mike tore the pole from a man's hand.

"Don't fool around with your tools!" Mike said fiercely. "Treat them the way you would a knife or a gun because they're just as deadly!"

As he watched the training of the newcomers, Rafer noted a difference between the other veterans and Mike—Mike was the only one who stressed to the novices the importance of the work they were doing.

"Don't think being strong means you can handle the ice," Rafer overheard Mike tell a group one morning. "That's like thinking any young, quick ballplayer can play for the Yankees. Icing is a skill, a craft, and you can't learn to do it well overnight. But if you work hard, learn to do it right, you'll join the company of some great men. I'm not saying they were famous or made a lot of dough, but they're men who are remembered and spoken of with respect in every railroad yard across the country!

"What if we don't want to become icemen, Mike?" A tall, blonde youth asked.

"Doesn't make a damn bit of difference!" Mike said brusquely. "Whatever work you do, that pride you felt in being a good iceman will help you! Pride in yourself earns the respect of others! That's what the hell its all about!"

On a night in late May, the day crews had finished their shift, and the locker room was a brawl of voices and laughter. Mike came from the locker room into the office, where Rafer was alone. Earl had left and Benny had phoned to say that his car, old and decrepit as Rafer's Ford, had broken down and he'd be late.

Mike slumped in a chair, weariness shadowing his face.

"It's the same story, year after year," he gestured in resignation toward the locker room. "A new bunch of yahoos showing up, balls full of juice, wanting only to screw and raise hell. Trying to get some savvy about icing into their heads is a waste of time."

"You and the others are doing all you can to help them learn."

"Not enough," Mike said gloomily. "A few weeks of training isn't enough. It takes that long just to make a guy understand how ice is never still, how it's always moving, and the ways a good iceman learns to use that movement." He paused. "By the time they gain a little savvy, it's time for them to move on." He sighed. "I've seen thousands of guys come through the Team Track, and I've never found one who might become a real iceman and want to stay! Honest to God, Rafer, before I die, I'd like to find just one!"

Two of the new workers, Jason and a companion named Link, swaggered into the office. Their faces were scrubbed and shining, heavy-buckled belts laced their lean waists, and both wore ornately brocaded cowboy boots.

"Hey, Mike, we're taking off now," Jason said. "You wanna come over to the Pink Garden and celebrate with us?"

"Celebrate what?" Mike asked scornfully. "Celebrate the way you two guys stumble around on the cars like three-legged goats? Celebrate that every time you hoist a block of ice, you're risking rupturing your balls? What the hell you got to celebrate?"

"We're young, real pretty, and primed to bring joy into a poor whore's heart!" Jason laughed. Link grinned in agreement.

"You're young, stupid, and primed to poke yourselves senseless," Mike growled.

"How about you, Rafer?" Jason smirked. "The Pink Garden has plenty of girls to go around."

"I'm waiting for Benny. I'm not sure how soon he'll be in."

"When Benny gets here, come on over. If he don't come, we can send one of the boys back to spell you for an hour. If you're a fast enough driller, that should be plenty of time."

"Get the hell out of here," Mike waved them away. "Tell that crap to Earl in the morning."

"I'm not afraid of Earl!" Jason blustered.

"I know, I know!" Mike snickered. "A stud like you isn't afraid of anyone. When old Earl levels a blast at you, you'll just wet your pants for the hell of it."

After the two youths had gone, Mike turned to Rafer.

"If you were looking for company some night, Rafer," Mike said quietly, "stay away from the Pink Garden. I know another place, the Olympia Club, on Jackson, a few blocks west of Halsted. The girls are a little older, but they appreciate kindness, and they don't order fancy, expensive drinks. Aunt Cora who runs the place is a fair old dame. I've been going there for years, I know its clean, and you won't get cheated."

"I got other things on my mind right now, Mike."

"Good enough," Mike said. He rose to leave and noticed the book at one side of Rafer's desk.

"What you reading, Rafer?"

"The Dialogues of Plato," Rafer said. "He's an ancestor of yours."

"I heard about him." Mike paused. "I got to admit, Rafer, I've never been much of a reader. An uncle I worked for when I first came from Crete didn't believe in school. An old cook in the kitchen where I washed dishes helped me or I wouldn't even be able to read and write." He picked up the book and leafed through the pages. "I guess this Plato must have been pretty smart."

"He was a famous philosopher who studied questions like 'what is truth' and 'what is justice.'"

"If you're reading books like this, Rafer," Mike said, "you got to be damn smart too."

"I've done too many stupid things in my life to think of myself as smart," Rafer said. "But I used to be a high school teacher, and I've always been a good reader."

"You were a teacher?" Mike seemed impressed. "Tell you the God's truth, Rafer, I feel a little ashamed because I'm Greek and I've never read Plato or any of those other famous Greeks. You've read their books, and I don't know anything about them." A pensiveness entered his voice. "Maybe we could talk about Plato sometime. You could fill me in on the things he writes about."

"Anytime you wanted, Mike. Plato offers us advice on how to live with good sense."

"That'd be great," Mike said. "Maybe somebody should get a copy of Plato to Old Harry in the White House and to that crazy yahoo in the Kremlin. Maybe he'll help them find a way to end this damn cold war before we all get blown to hell."

"The ancient Greeks were wise about many things," Rafer said, "but they also fought senseless wars against one another. Athens, one of the city-states, fought another Greek state, Sparta, until both were nearly destroyed."

"I thought ancient Greeks only fought Persians, and modern Greeks the damn Turks," Mike shrugged. "I guess when you come down to it, Greeks can make the same stupid, human mistakes as everybody else."

"Now you're philosophizing."

"How about that?" Mike grinned. "I guess it's in my blood!"

He paused at the door.

"You're doing fine, Rafe," he said quietly. "You're a decent man, and you treat the men fair. You're taking hold real good."

Mike's praise pleased Rafer more than if it had come from anyone else at the Team Track.

Among the young men who came to work at the Team Track

that spring was a drifter in his early thirties. Earl hired him and he went on the payroll as S.K. Nazim.

Rafer first noticed him across the crowded locker room because he loomed several inches taller than the tallest of the other men. Something else different about him was his long black hair, which he wore hanging past his shoulders or at other times tied in a flowing ponytail at the back of his head.

S.K.—the men called him by his initials—had been working at the Team Track for about a week when he came into the office with icing slips for Earl.

Seeing S.K. up close for the first time, Rafer noted his strong, hawklike face, his dark eyes, and his high-boned cheeks the shade of dark green olives. In addition to his imposing height, he had powerful shoulders and muscular arms, his upper body tapering down to a lean, hard waist. Rafer was reminded of the statues of victorious athletes in ancient games he'd seen in museums.

S.K. waited before Earl's desk until the straw boss looked up.

"Stamps told me to give you these slips, boss," S.K. said. On the surface his voice was quiet, and the word *boss* came casually from his lips, but his dark eyes seemed mocking and irreverent.

"They all here?"

"All here, boss."

Earl glared at him, perhaps sensing the mockery that Rafer detected. S.K. never wavered in meeting Earl's gaze.

"Any ice left on the truck?" Earl asked brusquely.

"Half dozen blocks."

"Be damn sure you unload them back into the big house."

S.K. nodded and left the office.

"Only faggots wear their hair that long," Earl muttered. "There's something else about the sonofabitch aggravates me . . . I can't put my finger on it, but I'll be watching him . . ."

In the first week in June, Rafer had a forewarning of what summer at the Team Track would be like. The weather suddenly turned hot, and a scorching wind blew across the hill. As quickly as the blocks of ice were dragged out of the big house, they began to melt, streams of water pouring over the tailgate of the trucks to the roadway.

In the stifling office, the phones rang continuously with calls from the yardmasters about cars to be iced. As many as fifteen crews at a time were icing at the yards and returning to reload. The worn wood floor of the office shook as a column of trucks rumbled up and down the hill, their wheels splashing through potholes flooded with water.

The melting ice seemed to drive Earl into a frenzy. While Rafer answered the phones, Earl spent most of his time on the hill. He met each truck returning from the yards and handed the drivers the icing slips, snarling at them to reload quickly and get rolling again.

Salvatore, aided by another mechanic, struggled mightily to repair the old trucks that kept breaking down. Despite his efforts, there were always at least half a dozen disabled in the garage. Several times during the day, Earl left the hill and stormed into the garage to rage at Salvatore for not getting the disabled trucks back into service more quickly.

"I'm not God!" Salvatore cried once in outrage to Rafer when Earl returned to the hill. "We got a dozen trucks should have been sold for junk years ago! Does he think I'm God?"

When Earl came back into the office from the hill, his beefy face was wet, his shirt glued like a second skin to his chest and shoulders. At those times, his gargantuan body gave off a stench of sweat that Rafer found overpowering.

Hard as he tried, Rafer couldn't find any redemptive decency in Earl's nature. When the straw boss wasn't snarling or cursing, he'd sit brooding silently at his desk. Rafer wondered what anger and bitterness filled his thoughts.

The onslaught of hot weather kindled a thirst in Rafer that couldn't be appeased by water or soft drinks. A score of times during the day, his lips dry and his throat parched, he thought with longing of a mug of cold beer.

He hadn't had a drink in almost four months. He had rarely

remained sober that long since leaving home, and that made him nervous. He felt a pressure building in his chest, his heart palpitating so wildly, he felt he might be having an attack.

Once, while Earl was arguing on the phone with a yardmaster, Rafer fled from the office to his car. He drove down the hill to the nearest tavern on Halsted. He parked outside and sat for a while in his car, clutching the wheel so hard his knuckles turned white. He thought of Mellie and Rosie, his heart wrenched with love. He also thought of how angry Earl would be if he detected Rafer had been drinking.

Rafer finally turned his car around and drove back up to the office, uncertain whether his fear of Earl or his love for his family had sent him back to the Team Track still dry.

In an effort to gain some support for his struggle, Rafer located an Alcoholics Anonymous group that met in the basement of Old St. Pat's Church in downtown Chicago. After work each night for a week, he went directly to the AA meetings. He listened to the confessions of others until his turn came.

"My name is Rafer Martin, and I'm an alcoholic . . ."

He tried to speak honestly of his addiction and his hope that he might stop.

Sitting in the meetings, joined to the anguish of others who were afflicted, he felt that he would be able to hold out. Back alone in his room, the sounds and smells of the summer night surging through his window, his fear returned. In his letters to Mellie, he tried to conceal his growing panic.

On an evening near the end of that week of fierce heat, Mike and Mendoza came into the office after Earl had left.

"How come you're still here, Rafer?" Mike asked.

"Benny's car broke down again."

"Like everything else is breaking down," Mendoza shook his head in disgust. "Salvatore is right about the damn trucks needing to be junked. I was at the I.C. yesterday, coming to a crossing when the brakes on 217 gave out. I'm pumping like crazy as I skid across the tracks . . . if a damn train had been coming, you'd be grieving at my funeral!"

"Can't we buy new trucks?" Rafer asked.

Mike and Mendoza both laughed.

"The last time we got a new truck," Mike said, "I think Coolidge was president."

"If they're breaking down now," Mendoza said, "wait and see what the hell happens in July and August."

Mike cut him off impatiently.

"I didn't come in to bitch about the trucks, Rafe," he said. "I wanted to ask about that new guy, S.K."

"He's brought slips into Earl a few times." Rafer said. "He looks big and strong."

"We got other big, strong guys here who are lousy icemen," Mike said. "He's been working with Stamps, who thinks he's got real ability."

"That isn't all he's got," Mendoza said brusquely. "He's got brass enough for a dozen men. Been a long time since I met anyone so goddam cocky,"

"He told Stamps he's never iced before, but Stamps doesn't believe him," Mike said. "Now, Mendoza is right, there's a lot of cockiness about him. But I've seen brassy yahoos before, and sometimes they can change." He paused. "Rafer, how about scheduling him to work with me for a few days?"

"You know Earl assigns the crews," Rafer said. "But I'll try, Mike. I'll put him on with you and shift Fenner over to Stamps. Earl will probably switch him back soon as he finds out."

"By then maybe I'll see for myself what the guy can do." Mike started from the office. "Thanks, Rafer."

"I wouldn't want the sonofabitch on my truck," Mendoza said as he followed Mike out the door.

After Benny arrived, complaining bitterly about the heat and the condition of his car, Rafer drove back to his hotel. His cramped room was airless, his window fan useless against the heat.

He fled from his room and walked along Halsted Street. Every tavern he passed was crowded with boisterous men and women, laughing and drinking. He felt a pervasive loneliness, as if he were suddenly isolated from all other human beings. He tried to rationalize taking a single drink to moisten the dryness in his throat. He had heard that there were AA groups in Sweden and Norway that believed the best method to conquer alcohol addiction was by moderate drinking.

As his thirst and craving grew, so did his fear that the months he'd remained sober could be swept away with the first drink. As his panic grew, he located a phone and called his AA support, Kelly, a retired postal worker he'd met at one of the meetings. Kelly spoke to him reassuringly, telling him to drink plenty of coffee. They arranged to meet in the Calypso lunchroom on Van Buren.

The interior of the lunchroom was as hot as the street despite several large ceiling fans whipping muggy air across a row of stools and tables. The fans also circulated the steamy odors of hamburger being grilled by a burly cook with a soiled apron tied around his waist.

When the skinny, sweating waitress came to his table, Rafer ordered black coffee. He drank one cup and ordered another. As he finished his second cup, Kelly and a woman entered the lunchroom. They spotted Rafer in the corner and came to his table.

Kelly was stocky and short, gray-haired with an earnest face. The woman he introduced to Rafer as Leota was about forty, slim-bodied with light hair and pale cheeks.

"We know what you're going through," Kelly spoke in a low, sympathetic voice. "You were right to have called."

"I think it's the heat," Rafer said. "My throat is dry and water or coke doesn't seem to help."

"The heat makes it harder," Kelly agreed. "All the more reason you got to be on your guard."

For the next half hour, Kelly spoke, sensibly and reassuringly, reaffirming his support, offering encouragement. Rafer kept nodding and, from time to time, expressing his resolve to stay dry.

He couldn't help feeling a sickly shame at his weakness, his inability to control his longing. He was conscious of the three of them huddled in the tawdry surroundings of the lunchroom. The grill man and waitress stared at them as if suspicious that their whispering involved some aberration.

After a while, Rafer found he wasn't listening to Kelly any longer, his thoughts focused on the woman.

She wasn't very pretty, but there was something about her that he found empathetic. He felt it was her eyes, shaded between blue and green and luminous in the pale circles of her cheeks. Sensitive and sad, they suggested to Rafer that she had been through hell herself. In the few instances she spoke, he learned she also had a room in the Poinsettia Hotel.

"I've never seen you there," Rafer said.

"I don't spend much time in my room. Mostly, I use it just to sleep."

The three of them rose to leave. Kelly clasped Rafer's hand tightly in both of his hands.

"Honest to God, Rafer, I'm glad you called," he said fervently. "That tells me you really want to make it. Remember you're not alone. Any time of the day or night, you call me or Leota, we'll be here for you."

Rafer thanked him and paid the check.

Outside the lunchroom, Kelly told them good-night. Rafer and Leota started walking back to the hotel together.

For a little while they didn't speak. Around them, the city moved sluggishly in the heat. Cars with open windows rumbled along Halsted, the blare of music trailing in their wake. Restless, gesturing men and women pushed by them on the street.

Leota asked him where he worked, and Rafer told her a little about the Team Track.

"I never thought about railroad cars needing to be iced," she said.

"I didn't know anything about this business either before I started working," Rafer said. "What about you? What work do you do?"

"I'm a part-time librarian at the branch library over on Morgan."

A police car with blaring siren raced by on Halsted. A few blocks away, another siren picked up the wail.

"How long have you had the problem," Rafer asked.

"Since I was a teenager," she said quietly. "It started in high school. I was a cheerleader . . ." she looked at him as if to see whether he found that believable. "At our parties . . . the football players would bring flasks of whiskey. I developed a taste . . ."

In the hotel lobby, the wizened old clerk at the desk fanning himself with a broken straw fan handed them their keys. Rafer's room was on the fourth floor, and Leota's one floor below. Rafer held the elevator door for her.

"You're on the floor with the first class rooms," Leota said. "You have your own bath."

"I share it with another fellow."

"That's better than sharing with a whole floor. We've got one poor old woman with digestive problems who sits in the toilet for an hour at a time."

"Come upstairs and use mine, if you like."

"That's kind of you, but I better not."

The elevator reached the third floor and the door opened.

"Maybe we could have a cup of coffee together sometime," Rafer said as Leota stepped out into the hallway.

"Sure. And like Kelly said, anytime you just want to talk, call me."

Rafer had one final glimpse of her pale face and sad eyes before the door closed.

Later that night, Rafer lay naked in a pool of sweat, unable to sleep, listening to the droning of the fan in his window. His craving for a drink had passed, but the heat kept him restless. He recalled his months of wandering. With all his energies spent fighting the drink, his thoughts dwelling on Mellie and Rosie, he had little inclination for any kind of relationship. There had been a few women to whom he had been attracted because he was lonely, but he had never betrayed Mellie. Now, for the first time in months, he felt a longing for the touch of another human being.

He knew it was because of the sad-eyed librarian. He imagined her body as it might look naked, slim-boned, lean-hipped, small-breasted. If they made love, he wondered, would it ease her sadness.

He looked at the clock beside the bed, its ghostly-green dial showing half past one. He sighed because he still had a long, wakeful night ahead of him.

Finally, he rose and turned on the lamp with the thin parchment shade. He took the snapshot of Mellie and Rosie from the top of the bureau and placed it close to him on the bed. With his notepad on his knees, he began a letter to his family.

My dearest Mellie and Rosie:

It is late at night and I'm getting ready to sleep. I am looking at your picture and imagine how much bigger Rosie must be getting now. With all my heart I hope that before long I'll hold both of you in my arms again. Meanwhile, since I'll be here at the hotel for a while, send me more photos.

The weather here has suddenly turned hot. The Team Track has gotten busy and the men are working hard. I've written you about Earl before and he is even meaner in the heat. But he doesn't bother me. I am doing my work and keeping busy.

Try not to worry about me. It has been almost three months now since I finished with the drying-out program and I haven't had a drink. I know that still isn't long enough to let me feel confident that I have licked the demon but it's a beginning. I keep thinking of both of you as my reward if I can beat this now.

He stared at the lines he had written and then at the picture and felt tears blur his eyes. He resumed writing.

Tell your mother and father I send them my love. Hug Rosie for me. I love you, Mellie. That's the most I can tell you now. But I am hopeful . . . I am hopeful.

Love,

Rafer

He folded the letter and inserted it into the envelope, sealed it, and affixed a stamp above the address. He put it on his bureau to mail first thing in the morning.

He shut off the lamp and returned to bed. The multicolored light from the window reflected across the small envelope. He carried it like a talisman with him into his sleep.

6

Mike

THE DAY AFTER MIKE HAD SPOKEN TO RAFER about assigning the new man to his truck, S.K. came to his locker. The room was noisy with the clatter of metal doors and the voices of men changing for work. S.K., muscular and long-haired, loomed a head taller than Mike.

"Schedule says I'm working with you, boss."

"You got any beef with that?"

"Work is work," S.K. shrugged.

Stamps, standing at his locker nearby, said, "You work with Mike, you working with the best damn iceman in the world."

"How come I'm so lucky?" S.K. motioned at the crowded locker room. "How come you didn't pick one of them?"

"Who gets picked doesn't matter," Mike said brusquely. "We like to switch new guys around on the trucks. You ready?"

S.K. nodded, and the two men left the locker room and walked up the hill to the trucks without speaking. Mike swung up into the cab and drove to the big house platform. S.K. joined him and they loaded the truck with the blocks of ice. On their way down the hill, they stopped at the garage to load on bags of salt.

Mike drove to their first stop at the I.C. yards. The cab windows were open, and the early morning air, already thick with heat, rushed in across their faces.

"You ever iced before?" Mike asked.

"Never knew anything about icing before I started."

"Stamps says you do it real good."

"I pick things up quick," S.K. shrugged. "He tells me you been doing it a long time."

"Yeah, a long time."

"I thought all Greeks went into restaurants." Mike caught a trace of a smirk on S.K.'s face.

"Not this Greek," Mike snapped. "To hell with restaurants."

They rode the rest of the way to the yard in silence. Mike stopped at the yardmaster's shanty for the location of the cars. Afterwards, he drove to the siding and parked alongside the first car.

They rode the HiLift platform to the top of the railroad car, then lowered the ramp from the truck to the bunkers. Mike opened the bunker plugs and checked the levels.

"They only need topping off," he said, "Maybe six to eight hundred pounds in each one."

S.K. dragged the first block from the truck across the ramp. The ice melting quickly in the heat soaked the roof of the car with water, but he moved on the slippery surface with sureness and agility. Swinging his pick, he cut the block rapidly into a half dozen chunks that he grasped with his tongs and threw into the bunkers. He swiftly cut down a second block and tossed those chunks into the bunkers, as well.

While some of S.K.'s movements were erratic and there were things he was doing wrong, Mike was impressed. The man was quick and strong, but that was true of others at the Team Track. What Mike saw in S.K. was a confidence and an instinctive sense of timing in handling the ice. Men could ice for years and never develop the fluid, swift motion S.K. had achieved after only a few weeks.

"You sure you never iced before?" Mike asked again because he found it hard to believe.

S.K. shook his head.

After icing and salting the bunkers at the other end of the car, Mike drove to a second car where the bunkers were almost empty and needed about four thousand pounds apiece.

S.K. opened the plugs. Mike dragged the ice across the ramp, held the four-hundred-pound block balanced in his tongs for an instant, and then released it. When the falling block struck the bunker, it split evenly in half, each two-hundred-pound chunk dropping neatly into one of the bunkers.

S.K. had been watching him closely and let loose a low whistle.

"I guess, boss, that's why they call you number one."

A barely veiled mockery was still in his voice.

Mike suppressed his irritation. He continued cutting the blocks so they split and fell neatly into the bunkers. Within the space of several minutes, both bunkers were full. Afterwards, S.K. shoveled in salt and closed the plugs.

Mike walked the runway to the other end of the car, and S.K. joined him.

"How about letting me try this one, boss?" Without waiting for Mike's reply, S.K. gripped a block with his tongs and dragged it across the ramp. Imitating Mike's movements, he held the block suspended for an instant in his tongs and then let it fall. It struck the bunker's rim and splintered into several large chunks that skidded off the runway to shatter on the ground.

S.K. bristled in aggravation. He moved quickly to drag a second block from the truck, held it an instant, and let it fall. When the block struck the rim, several smaller pieces tumbled into the bunkers while larger chunks slid off the roof once again to shatter on the ground.

"You don't learn to ice in a couple of weeks," Mike said quietly.

S.K. said nothing, but his eyes glared defiance. Mike couldn't understand the reason for the man's hostility, which continued to irritate him.

After finishing at the I.C., they drove to the Grand Trunk yards where they waited an exasperating hour for the yardmaster, who claimed he couldn't locate the car. Meanwhile, in the blistering midday heat, the ice melting on the truck formed large puddles of water around the wheels.

"You're supposed to spot the damn car before you call us!" Mike said angrily to the yardmaster when they finally got the location. "What the hell you trying to pull?"

The yardmaster shrugged and turned away.

"He didn't tell us where that damn car was on purpose" Mike muttered to S.K. as they left the shanty. "The sonofabitch has it in for Earl and makes us pay for it."

After they'd finished icing the car, they drove back to the Team Track to reload.

The midday sun on the roof of the truck made the cab an oven, and Mike felt his energy whipped by the heat. S.K. didn't appear bothered by the work or heat. He sat impassively, sweat glistening on the powerful muscles of his neck and arms. He reached up to brush back the long, loose strands of his hair.

"Doesn't that hair bother you?"

"Doesn't bother me, summer or winter."

Mike knew S.K. was only a few years older than his son, Lucas, who would be twenty that year. He allowed himself to imagine that Lucas might have grown up to be as tall and strong as the young man beside him. Perhaps, if he had inherited Mike's kinship with the ice, he might have been as agile and quick as S.K.

At the top of the Team Track hill, Mike pulled up before the big house, and he and S.K. reloaded the truck. As they climbed back into the cab, another HiLift rumbled up the hill. Noodles stuck his head out the cab window.

"Fat man's in the road raising hell with every crew," Noodles scowled. "I was gonna run over the bastard but was afraid I'd wreck my truck!"

Mike waved and drove down the hill to where Earl waited outside the office. Mike stopped the truck beside him, keeping the engine idling, and handed Earl the icing slips.

Earl's face was soaked with sweat, his shirt glued to his body, his barrel chest heaving with his labored breathing.

"What took you so damn long at the Grand Trunk?"

"Yardmaster didn't spot the car."

"You been around long enough not to let him pull that shit on you!" Earl snapped. "You probably lost several thousand pounds!"

Earl looked past Mike at S.K. He seemed about to ask why they were working together, but Mike quickly shifted gears and gunned the truck forward. The motor's roar drowned out Earl's voice.

"Don't pay attention if Earl bitches at you," Mike said. "He bitches at everyone."

S.K. stared out the window and didn't answer.

As they worked through the afternoon, Mike pointed out ways that S.K. could improve cutting and throwing the ice. He was pleased and impressed once again at how quickly S.K. applied his advice. Putting aside his annoyance at the man's hostility, Mike couldn't help feeling a growing excitement at S.K.'s ability and promise. Stamps had been right about the man's natural ability.

Yet, as the day wore on, battling the heat and his weariness, Mike grew more irritated by the surliness and insolence in S.K.'s attitude and tone. Each time he called Mike, "boss," the mockery in his voice was evident.

Mike's aggravation grew and fueled his temper. After they'd iced a fruit car in an isolated corner of the Santa Fe yards, he couldn't restrain himself any longer.

"Goddamit, you listen to me now!" he confronted S.K. angrily. "You're doing the work, but everything else says you don't give a damn! You call me 'boss,' but you're telling me to go fuck myself! Now you're younger and maybe stronger, but if you don't start behaving like a real partner, by God, you and me are going to have it out!"

His rage rolling through him in waves, Mike clenched his fists and fully expected to fight the younger, bigger man.

S.K. stared down at him and seemed surprised at his outburst.

"You're one tough little Greek," S.K. said calmly. "I bet you'd put up a hell of a scrap. But I'm not going to fight you now because you called it right. When I say 'boss,' that's not what I'm thinking."

"I don't give a good goddam what you're thinking! You just show a little respect, and when you talk to me, Mike's my name!"

"Okay," S.K. shrugged. "Mike it is."

After that initial confrontation, they worked together more amicably for the balance of the week. S.K. still didn't display any friendliness, but he worked more diligently. Mike drove him hard and all week long kept up a barrage of advice.

"Hold the tongs a few inches to the right of the block," he said. "Give them a little twist when you let the ice go."

Later, he issued S.K. a warning.

"You got your feet too close together," he said. "Keep them fifteen, eighteen inches apart. If the block falls, it's got room to land between them."

He criticized the way S. K. lifted the blocks of ice.

"You're not bending your knees!" Mike said sharply. "You're hoisting the ice with your back! If you're off balance or make the wrong move, you can tear up your back muscles! Your leg muscles are stronger! Use your legs!"

At times, his zeal to teach the younger man overcame his patience.

"Not that way!" he growled. "How many times I got to tell you to hold your pike pole lower when you strike the block!"

"Goddamit, I'm holding it that way!"

"I'm telling you you're doing it wrong!"

"You're sure as hell hard to please!" S.K. said heatedly.

"Don't do a damn thing to please me!" Mike said. "Do it because you want to be the best! That's how a man should work! Be the goddam best!"

Once, after a heated exchange between them, S.K. threw down his tongs with a curse.

"The whole damn week I'm doing this wrong and doing that wrong!" S.K. said angrily. "Who the hell made you master of the ice? You must think you're some kind of god!"

"I'm not God," Mike said quietly. "I'm just an iceman. But if you want to learn to ice, you watch me and you listen."

Even as he sought to pass on to the younger man the knowledge of the work he'd acquired through the years, he tried to convey his passion about the icing, as well.

"I'll never forget my first day on the job," he said as they were driving between yards on Friday of that week. "The foreman handed me a shovel and told me to transfer salt from the salt pit onto the conveyer. When he came back a few hours later, I had shoveled forty ton. He couldn't believe I had done that much alone and, next day, he made me helper on a truck." He glanced at S.K. "All I'm saying is a man should bring that kind of energy and spirit to his work."

He also spoke about the icemen he'd worked with.

"Israel and Pacheco were champions!" Mike said fervently. "When the two of them were icing cars, yardmasters, brakemen, and engineers all came to watch. I swear to God, they were like great athletes! They could ice a dozen cars at a stretch from the top of a moving truck, never stumble, never miss a bunker, never let a chunk of ice fall the wrong way!" As Mike spoke, he gripped the wheel so hard his knuckles whitened. "I tried to make myself like them, the way a rookie hitter would try to imitate DiMaggio. I watched them and practiced, tried to do what they did and feel what they felt."

He paused, suddenly concerned because S.K. might think he was babbling.

"I didn't mean to bend your ear," he said gruffly. "I get carried away sometimes."

Late Friday afternoon, at the end of their week together, Mike drove up the Team Track hill. The sun had settled behind the skyline of the downtown buildings that loomed like pillars of fire on the horizon.

Despite the heat, all week Mike had driven himself hard to set an example for S.K. He was more tired than he'd felt in a long time, his muscles aching, his back so sore it hurt him to take a breath. He longed for a bath to wash off his sweat and stink and then to stretch out on his bed, but he resolved to complete the week without showing any weakness. He worked briskly beside S.K. to transfer the ice left on the truck back into the big house.

Afterwards, he parked his truck alongside the other HiLifts and swung down from the cab as S.K. climbed down from the platform. They started down the hill and Mike caught S.K.'s arm.

"Hold on a minute, S.K.," he began quietly. "There's something I want to tell you." He struggled for the right words. "I know I been driving you hard all week about ways to ice and bending your ear with stories about the old days." He shook his head ruefully. "You got a right to be pissed. But I only did it because you got natural talent. I swear to God, I've seen guys ice for years who don't handle themselves the way you do now. That's why I been driving you . . . I think you'd make a hell of an iceman, good as anyone I've ever seen since Israel and Pacheco."

S.K. stared at him for a moment in silence. In the falling twilight, Mike couldn't see his face clearly. Then, without a word, S.K. swung around and started down the hill. After he'd gone a short distance, he turned abruptly and came striding back to where Mike stood.

"Goddam, you're really something!" he taunted Mike. "I mean, you should get a prize for being so stupid!"

Mike was stunned and then outraged. He took a threatening step toward S.K. who waved him back.

"I'm not going to fight you now," S.K. said scornfully, "so don't swell up like a bantam rooster who's been clawed. You can't help being Greek but you can help being stupid! All that garbage about the ice! You carry on like its gold! It's ice, for God's sake, dirty, frozen water! I wouldn't give a shit about the damn ice even if you weren't Greek and if I wasn't a Turk!"

Mike stared at him in disbelief.

"What the hell you mean a Turk?"

"A Turk!" S.K. snapped. "You know what a Turk is, don't you?"

"I know what a Turk is!" Mike cried. "What the hell you been hiding it for? Why didn't you come right out and say you're a Turk! You ashamed of it?"

"I wasn't hiding anything!" S.K. said harshly. "You never asked me. I use S.K. because my name is a choker. Suleiman Khalid Nazim! "

"If that's your name, use it!"

"Is Mike your name? What the hell was it in Greek?"

"That's different!"

"The hell it is!"

Mike stared at him, seething because he felt deceived and because he had been foolish enough to pin all his hopes on a Turk.

"All right!" he cried. "You're a Turk! Well, I got bad memories of Turks from my village! Turks stole land that belonged to my family and to other Cretans!"

"Bullshit!" S.K. snarled. "I've heard that stuff about Turks stealing other people's land since I was a kid! My people belonged on that land before any of you! Look into your own Bible! When Abraham settled his family in the land of Canaan, the Hittites, the ancestors of the Turkish people, were already living there. Your Bible says that Abraham bought land from Hittites for his wife Sarah's grave and for his own grave."

"I'm not talking about all that Bible stuff!" Mike said vehemently, "I'm talking about the Turks who came into our village in Crete to loot and steal! My sister and I had to hide in the fruit cellar when drunken Turks rioted outside our house! And what about the things Turks did to Cretan women and children! That's what the hell I'm talking about!"

"Greeks committed atrocities against Turkish women and children, as well!"

"The hell you say!"

"Take your head out of the ice long enough to learn something about the Greek wars against the Turks! They attacked Turkish towns and massacred everyone, including the women and children!"

"I don't believe that shit!"

"What the hell do you know?" S.K. cried. "I don't know why I'm bothering to argue with you! You said to hell with restaurants! What kind of a Greek says to hell with the way all of his people make a living! Who ever heard of a Greek iceman? Maybe you're not even Greek!"

"I'm Greek, goddamit!" Mike raged. "You better believe I'm Greek and damn proud of it!"

A truck rumbled past them up the hill, its lights flashing across their faces. As if the lights prompted both men to understand the absurdity of the exchange, S.K. turned suddenly and with a final scornful gesture of his hand stalked down the hill.

Mike struggled for a final biting salvo.

"From now on I'm calling you Suleiman!" he cried loudly. "Suleiman! So everyone will know you're a goddam Turk!"

At the beginning of the weekend, Mike spent Saturday morning in bed resting. In spite of having worked hard all week, he had slept fitfully the night before. His confrontation with the Turk seethed in his head and kept him awake.

Later in the morning, he listened to music on the radio to distract himself. He felt calmer until he saw his still-angry face in the bathroom mirror.

"Why'd you waste time talking?" he cried at his reflection. "Why didn't you just punch the sonofabitch in his smart-aleck Turkish mouth!"

After shaving, he took a long bath, which helped relax him. He dressed in a clean shirt and light cotton jacket. For the first time all week, he touched his thick graying hair with a touch of pomade.

At twilight, on his way to his car, he bought flowers from a street vendor. Afterwards, he drove a half dozen blocks to the Olympia Club. He had been frequenting that brothel (he preferred the word to *whorehouse*) for years. He had started going there after becoming disgruntled with the simpering young girls at the other neighborhood brothel, the Pink Garden.

He walked up the steps of the brownstone building and rang the bell. A young Oriental maid let him in, and Aunt Cora, matronly, henna-haired, and heavily made-up, came through the velvet drapes to greet him with a kiss.

"I always know it's Saturday night when you show up with flowers, Mike," she said warmly.

"Aunt Cora, I can't start my weekend any other way," Mike smiled.

"Something to drink, honey?" she took his arm. "How about a glass of wine and a dish of Mattie's tasty cheese and ham appetizers?"

"Maybe later, Aunt Cora."

She led him through the drapes into a large parlor where half a dozen women in negligees reclined around the room. Several wore black silk stockings with black garter belts. As Mike had told Rafer in the office, most were a few years older than the girls in the Pink Garden.

During the years he'd been coming to the brothel, Mike had had sex with a number of the women, and they greeted him affectionately. Darlene and Beatrice fussed over him with hugs and kisses. Several other women preened themselves, waiting for him to make his selection.

"Don't get your hopes up, girls," Beatrice laughed. "Mike is bringing flowers for Dolores. Ever see another john do that?"

"He spends all his time with her," one of the women muttered. "It's not fair."

"Now, girls," Aunt Cora said reprovingly. "Jealously isn't seemly. Many of you have spent loving time with Mike. He's one of our favorites. Now we shouldn't resent that he's gotten comfortable with Dolores." She turned to Mike. "She's upstairs waiting for you. You know her room."

Mike passed through velvet drapes and walked up the stairs. He stopped before a door numbered "10" and knocked gently. Dolores called an answer, and he entered the room.

He was caught at once by the familiar aromas of powder and perfume, a tantalizing scent he always associated with Dolores. When he had once asked her about it, she laughed and told him the scent was of sin.

Despite the heat outside, the windowless room, sheltered by layers of mortar, wood, and drapes from the sun, was cool. In the center stood a large bed. On either side were lamps with satin shades that cast a soft, shaded light. In the corner was a metal sculpture of a dancer, legs poised in a pirouette and arms extended gracefully toward the sky. Behind the statue, a velvet drape concealed a bathroom.

Dolores emerged from behind the drape.

"I've been expecting you, Mike." Dolores's low, melodious voice was pleasing to his ear. She walked from the shadows into lamplight, her negligee unfolding about her naked thighs, and gave him a hug and an affectionate kiss.

He handed her the flowers with a flourish.

"They're lovely, Mike," she smiled. "You're the only man I ever knew brings a whore flowers."

"Don't call yourself a whore!"

"Then what am I?"

"I've told you before," he said, "you're a lady of the evening."

"And you're a gentleman of the evening," Dolores said. She put the flowers into a slim vase that she filled with water from the basin behind the drape.

He had never found the courage to ask her age but guessed her to be in her early forties, her body revealing a transition from youth into middle age. A tracing of wrinkles were visible at her throat and around her brown eyes, which glowed in lamplight. She had a lovely face and chestnut-shaded hair that hung in luxuriant waves to her shoulders. While many of the women in the house had pendulous breasts, with nipples large as a man's thumbs, Dolores's breasts remained those of a younger woman, her nipples like glistening red grapes. Her body was slender, her belly firm, and her thighs tapered into long, willowy legs with fine veins faintly visible beneath her smooth skin.

For the last two years, Mike had slept only with Dolores. They had become as comfortable with one another as a husband and wife who'd been married for years. Indeed, they had grown so familiar that one night she'd revealed to him that her real name wasn't Dolores but Reba.

"Can you imagine a whore with a scrub woman's name like

Reba?" she sighed. "It has all the sexual appeal of a dishrag. If I'd kept that sad name, I'd have been on the street in a week."

He was grateful for her candor, believing it revealed her genuine affection for him. And he continued to call her Dolores.

What was pleasing about their relationship was that he no longer had to prove anything to her. She understood there were nights, more and more frequent, when his weariness desired companionship instead of sex.

His last few visits to Dolores had been spent resting and talking, so that night he felt impelled to seek the release of sex. He stripped to his shorts and lay on the bed beside her. But after they had caressed for a while, once again a weariness swept his body and he faltered. She sensed his drawing back and paused in her movements, as well.

"We don't have to do anything, honey," she said gently. "Just relax . . . relax. I'll get the lotion and give you a massage."

He had begun to enjoy her massages as much as the sex. He'd strip naked, recline on his belly, and extend his arms. She'd apply a creamy, lightly scented lotion to his flesh.

"You've got a wonderful back," she told him the first time she massaged him. "That's part of a man's body a woman doesn't usually see. Your back is solid with muscle and without an ounce of fat. If you saw the white and flabby bodies I usually see, you'd know what a treat it is for me to look at you."

In the beginning, he anticipated the massage would become erotic foreplay. His body tensed as he waited for the rehearsed motion, the practiced gesture. But all he felt was the cool lotion applied gently by her hands across his flesh. His limbs relaxed, his muscles yielding to her touch. After a while, he slept.

The first time he fell asleep after she massaged him, he woke with a start to see Dolores sitting nearby watching him. The lamplight reflected softly across her face and he caught a glimpse of the stunning beauty she must have been as a girl.

"How long have I been asleep?"

"Not long," she said. "About a half hour."

"You must think I'm a real peach," his embarrassment made

him speak gruffly. "Guy comes in for some humping and falls asleep."

"All I think is that you were tired," she said. "Besides, my massaging relaxed you. I got good hands for that."

He nodded in agreement and swung his legs off the bed. He dressed and pulled some bills from his pocket.

"You don't have to give me as much," she said. "I wouldn't take anything, but Aunt Cora will want her share."

"That's all right," he said, and as if to make amends for falling asleep, he put down more than he had ever given her before.

"That's too much, Mike."

"Forget it," he said. "I took up your time, and then I fell asleep."

He stood for a moment by the door. She must have glimpsed a hint of pity in his face.

"Don't feel sorry for me," she spoke with a sharper edge to her voice.

"I'm not feeling sorry for you," he said quietly. "You're probably sorry for me . . . this old guy who comes in for a hump and falls asleep. That's a good one."

"I'm not sorry for you," she said and came to the door. "I know what kind of man you are." She kissed him lightly on the cheek.

On his next few visits to the Olympia Club, Dolores massaged him again. After he'd stripped and lay naked on his belly, she rubbed his body from his neck and shoulders, and then along his legs to his ankles. Wherever her hands touched his flesh, his weariness was eased. Even when her palms stroked his buttocks, a touch that vibrated through his genitals, he felt no throbbing of desire.

On one of those visits, goaded by the suspicion that she might be amusing the other women with stories about the old man who came to be massaged and to sleep, he pressed her body back against the bed, roughly spread her legs and pounded into her. For a flurried moment he felt a surge of fire, and then it was over. Her face was close to his, and he saw her eyes, haunted and without pleasure. He understood then how the years of fucking had stripped the act of all feeling for her.

"I'm sorry," he said.

"I know," she said quietly. "It got to be too much . . . coming in and laying there while I massaged you. You had to show me you're a man . . . but I knew that the first time we made love."

He felt remorseful about his actions, which suddenly seemed childish. Before he left, he did something he had never done before. He reached down and raised her hand and gently kissed her fingers.

After that night, he relaxed and enjoyed the massage. He often slept afterwards. He woke to her close beside him, her warm flesh making him feel nested and content. In those reposeful moments, she spoke and he listened, finding her voice soothing.

Once she understood that he felt no resentment about all the men she had known, she talked of those men, big and small, bold and shy, and the dreams and fantasies they shared with her. Sex to him had always been a fairly simple matter of desire aroused and then released through coupling. He was astounded at her revelations of the world of fetish and bondage.

"My God!" he said, after one of her recitals. "If those yahoos had to put in a full day on a HiLift, believe me, they wouldn't have any energy left for that stuff!"

In the hours they spent together, he learned a good deal of brothel lore from Dolores. She told him how the term *red-light district* began back in the early railroad days in Kansas City. The brakemen would visit the whorehouses near the yards, hanging their red lantern signal lamps outside. It was the job of the dispatcher to send men out to warn the brakemen wherever a red lantern burned that their train was ready to pull out.

From Dolores, Mike learned, as well, that operating a brothel was like running a business. Furnishings had to be pleasing to the eye, laundry had to be sent out, connections had to be cultivated with politicians and police. Problems with the girls, treating their depression as well as counseling hygiene for them, had to be addressed. The brothel staff had to be supervised, arrangements made for food, liquor, and music. Finally, there was the importance of cultivating a cheerful environment. If the customers were happy, they came back. If they didn't, then, like any business, the brothel failed.

Dolores had worked in brothels in New Orleans and in Kansas City before coming to Chicago, and she spoke of Aunt Cora as the most caring madam she had ever known.

"Many of the madams treat their girls like meat," Dolores said, "but that's not true of Aunt Cora. Oh, there are times when she'll get angry and slap one of the girls for something she's done, but most of the time she's like a true mother, concerned with our welfare and keeping up our spirits. The girls love to hear her talk about the grand whorehouses she worked in at the turn of the century when she started. Aunt Cora told us how elegant the establishments were then, luxurious parlors with Venice glass over the gas jets, marble statues of nymphs and cupids, and drapes of blood-red velvet hanging from ceiling to floor. The clients at that time were influential politicians, judges, and wealthy businessmen who came not only to fuck but to talk, drink vintage wine, and smoke fine cigars."

Sometimes, Mike didn't really listen to what Dolores was saying. His spirit rose and fell on the pleasing waves of her voice. He'd drift in and out of sleep, dream briefly, wake to her reassuring presence.

Although he preferred to hear her speak rather than talk himself, he shared with her what he had never spoken about to anyone else, the loss of his wife and his son.

"I know what I did to my wife was wrong," Mike said. "A guy should marry or tomcat around. I tried to do both."

"Many more married men than single ones come to a whorehouse," Dolores said. "Sometimes their wives know and don't care. They're tired or they've got children to raise. They may not even care because it relieves them of the bother of sex with men they no longer love."

"I don't blame Natalie anymore," Mike said. "It was my fault because I wanted her and other women too. But what wasn't right was that she took my son away. He's a man now . . . a man, and I don't know if I'll ever see him again."

"It seems a cruel thing to do," Dolores said. "But when a woman is hurt bad, she'll do cruel and angry things. Maybe your wife will relent someday or perhaps your son will want to see you and come looking for you."

"I'd like to see my son" Mike said fervently "Any man, no matter what a bastard he's been, should have the right to see his son."

As much as they talked and as good a listener as he found Dolores to be, she found it difficult to understand his feeling for the icing. He tried a number of times, hoping that if she grasped that world, she'd know him better. But she could only envision men on trucks hurling chunks of ice into railroad cars. It was a job, one she accepted that Mike did better than any one else, but still just a job.

But on that June night, driven by a need to talk, he poured out his feelings about the growing effort it took to push his body through his days. He shared his anxiety about the icing machines that might end icing as he had known it for a lifetime. He also spoke about his confrontation with the Turk.

"You got to understand how Greeks and Turks feel about one another," Mike said, and recalling his showdown with Suleiman rekindled his outrage. "I tell you, I wouldn't give a damn about this guy now except for his ability! How do you like that? First time in thirty years I get a rookie who might make a great iceman, and he turns out to be a Turk!"

"Can you work with him?"

"I don't know," Mike said somberly. "But I can tell you he doesn't want to work with me. He hates Greeks! I felt that when he first joined me on the truck, even before I knew who he was. Now I got to be honest, when I found out he was a Turk, I swear to God it was like someone hit me in the head with a brick!"

From the rooms around them came the high-pitched voices of women and the hoarse laughter of men. Strains of jazz floated from the parlor downstairs.

"The girls here say that when a man's naked, you can't tell an Irishman from a German, or a Norwegian from a Pole," Dolores said quietly. "The way we remember men is whether they're gentle or rough, kind or cruel."

He admitted the truth in what she said, but his hatred of Turks, a feeling entrenched in him from childhood, defied reason.

Yet, when he thought about Dolores, he felt his emotions of hate overwhelmed by his feelings for her, an affection that had been growing stronger for months. He thought about her often during the day and longed to have her in bed beside him at night. He came finally, bewilderingly, to understand that the emotion he felt for her was love.

That awareness of love's power emboldened him, and that night, he spoke to her of something he'd been thinking about for months.

"Dolores," he said, and his voice was unsteady, "Dolores, I'm going to ask you something . . . and I want you to be honest with me. I been thinking about it for quite a while." He paused for a deep breath to ease the tightness in his chest. "I want us to be married," he said. "I want you to be my wife."

He saw her face suddenly raw with shock.

"Are you teasing me?" she asked, her voice shaken. "Is this a joke?"

"Teasing you?" He was amazed how she could think such a thing. "I'm damn serious! I'm asking you to marry me! I wouldn't joke about something like that!"

She pushed herself quickly and gracelessly off the bed, her negligee whipping about her thighs, and stood staring down at him. In the lamplight he couldn't see her eyes, but he felt their fire.

"I'm a whore!" the words came burned from her lips. "You've fucked me enough times to understand that! You're asking a whore to marry you!"

"I don't think of you like that, Dolores!" Mike said fervently. "I've come to care a great deal for you. Hell, don't you think I know what I'm saying?"

She shook her head vehemently.

"There isn't a man living who wouldn't resent what I've done with other men!" she said bitterly "You think it would be all right now, but a day would come when you'd start brooding about it, and you'd look at me like I was some kind of filth!"

"I wouldn't do that!" he protested.

"The hell you wouldn't!" she said, and he felt the whip of fury in her voice. "You'd remember suddenly the hundreds of men who'd used me, every part of me, every hill and hole. You'd hate me then!"

She turned away from him in a gesture of rejection, her own fear stronger than his assurances of love.

He rose from the bed and stood awkward and bewildered before her. He hadn't anticipated the violence of her reaction.

From a nearby room the strains of a harmonica carried through the hallway. For an instant the sound carried him back to some memory of his youth.

"Listen to me now, Dolores," he said earnestly. "I'm not talking about fucking. You and me have had more than enough of that to last us a lifetime. We can still do it, sometimes, but that's not what I'm talking about. That isn't the reason I want you to be my wife."

She stepped away from him, retreating into the shadows so he could no longer see her face.

"An old woman who lived alone died in my building last year," he said. "A week passed before anyone found her body. Then, just before Christmas, an old man, a German who sold used shoes on Maxwell Street, died alone in his apartment two floors below mine. They didn't find his body until the smell got real bad."

He heard her breathing, deep and slow.

"After the old man died," Mike said, "I started knocking on the doors of old people in our building I knew lived alone. Every few days I'd knock to check on them. But I had to stop . . ." He sighed. "One old lady called the cops because she thought I was planning to rob her."

Several people, talking loudly, passed in the hallway outside their door. A hand slapped bare flesh and a woman shrieked with laughter.

"I began thinking the most terrible thing that could happen

to someone would be to die alone," he said. "Maybe days passing before anyone finds your body. Now, each of us needs someone close . . . someone to be with, someone to be there if the end comes."

He was suddenly concerned Dolores might think that his fear of dying alone was the only reason he'd asked her to marry him.

"The most important reason I want you to be my wife is because I love you," he said quickly. "Honest to God, Dolores, I haven't said that to any woman in more than twenty years, but I'm saying it to you now."

For a long moment, she didn't respond, and he had a nagging feeling that he hadn't used the right words to convince her of his love.

Then a strange, tight sound emerged from her lips, and for a shattered moment, he thought she might be laughing at him. When she moved from the shadows into the light, he saw the tears on her cheeks.

"What you crying for?" he asked in shock because he had never seen her face tear stained before. "C'mon now," he said gently. "You crying because a battered old iceman is asking you to marry him?"

"That's not why I'm crying," she said in a low, husky voice. "I'm crying because I've come to love you too, Mike Zervakis. Aunt Cora would say the most stupid thing a whore can do is fall in love. But I love you. And I've been scared, waiting for that day when you'd grow tired of me, find a younger, prettier girl with a young girl's body. And all I'd have would be the memory of the good times we spent together."

Tears made her eyes seem larger and more intense. A strand of her hair had fallen loose about her temple, curled across her cheek.

"I've thought of growing old too," she said, "and not having anyone, an old childless whore . . . I've had five abortions, and while it seemed good sense each time, I often think of those unborn babies now. They might have grown up to love me and look after me so I wouldn't have to be alone."

She paused and he heard her quiet, sad voice echo from the hidden corners of the room.

"I often thought that was the way God would punish me for the life I've led," she said. "In the end he'd let me die alone in atonement for my sins. That's what I thought was going to happen. So you have to understand how hard I find it to believe you love me and want me as your wife."

"You better believe it!" Mike cried. "I wouldn't ask you if I didn't want us to spend the rest of our lives together! "

For a long moment she was silent, watching him, and he felt as if she were trying to peer into his heart.

She walked closer to him, took his hand, and raised it slowly to her cheek. Against the loveliness of her face he saw his hand as if for the first time, thick, blunt fingers, calloused knuckles, scarred palms. She kissed it tenderly.

"All right, Mike," she said quietly. "I don't know what's going to happen to us, but I love you too, and I don't have the strength to send you away. So if you're sure that's what you want . . . well, all right. I'll be the most happy woman of pleasure in the world to marry you and come live with you."

He was swept with a feeling of elation.

"Well, all right then!" he said jubilantly. "By God, all right then!"

He grabbed her and squeezed her hard. He was suddenly overwhelmed by knowing he'd have Dolores with him at night when he went to bed and in the morning when he woke. They'd eat their meals together and, in the evening, walk arm in arm along Halsted Street like other couples.

In that moment, the small windowless room remote from the world outside, the room draped in velvet and shaded in lamplight, became a cloister from which he'd begin the remainder of his life with a lover's pure heart.

7

Rafer

THE SWELTERING HEAT CONTINUED FOR ALMOST two weeks. All day long, loaded trucks driving to the yards and empty ones returning to reload rumbled up and down the Team Track hill. To replace the vast quantities of ice being used, several times a day, mammoth trailers from the manufacturing facility delivered ice to the big house.

Rafer spent the day in the stifling office, taking orders and trying to calm angry yardmasters calling to complain about trucks that hadn't arrived.

While Rafer answered the phones, Earl spent much of the day outside on the hill, passing slips to the men and shouting at them to keep the trucks rolling.

From time to time, a phone call for Earl came in from the ice company's main office. The voice on the line would say crisply "Downtown calling!" Rafer understood these calls were being relayed to Earl because a yardmaster or railroad superintendent had called downtown to complain about a delayed delivery.

When Rafer called Earl, the straw boss hurried into the office and nervously grasped the phone. Most of the time, he listened or offered a brief apology in a craven voice. "Every truck is on the road . . ." "I understand . . ." "We'll get on it right away . . ." Seeing the straw boss humbled, his voice trembling, Rafer couldn't help feeling pity for him. However, any sympathy he felt was dispelled soon after Earl was off the phone. As if the humiliation and rebukes he endured had to be passed on to others at once, when Earl returned to the hill, his shouts at the drivers became curses.

"You useless sons-a-bitches, keep them rolling! Farrell, move that goddam truck! Gries, you stupid bastard, your lift chain is dragging!"

The rumble of the trucks drowned out most of Earl's curses and shouts so it seemed to Rafer the straw boss was a sweat-drenched madman, railing and swearing to himself.

When the frenzy of activity quieted for a while, Earl came into the office. He turned the old floor fan toward his desk and sat in its draft, his face red and his breathing labored. Rafer worked tensely, waiting for him to find any excuse to explode.

On Friday, after S.K. had been working with Mike for a week, Earl came into the office from the hill and grabbed the work schedule off his desk. He waved it angrily at Rafer.

"Was it you or Benny put S.K. on with Mike?"

"I did, Earl." Rafer felt his heart pounding.

"Who the hell told you to do it?"

"Nobody told me, Earl."

Earl glared at him. "Any scheduling involves Mike, you talk to me first. Understand?"

Rafer nodded.

"I got some good reports on that long-haired bastard," Earl said. "Several of the yardmasters been asking for him. I'm giving him his own truck. Take number 27 away from that useless sonofabitch, Malvolo, and give it to S.K."

Rafer had never heard Earl praise anyone before, and that confirmed Mike's feelings about the new man.

"Who do you want me to put on Mike's truck?

"Give him Malvolo."

Later that same evening, after Earl had gone and Rafer and Benny were in the office, the door burst open and Mike stormed in. His face reflected a fury Rafer had never seen before.

"Did you guys know about the sonofabitch?" Mike cried.

Benny stared at Mike in shock. Rafer sat in bewildered silence.

"I'm talking about S.K.! Except his name isn't S.K. His name is Suleiman! Suleiman something-or-other! The sonofabitch is a Turk!"

"A Turk!" Incited by Mike's anger, Benny uttered the word as if it were a disease. "Jesus Chris', a Turk!"

"I only knew him by his initials, Mike," Rafer said, "He went on the payroll that way."

"The balls of the guy!" Mike said hoarsely. "Comes in for a job and doesn't tell anyone he's a goddam Turk! He's ashamed! And he goddam well should be ashamed!"

"A Turk!" Benny spit out the word.

Mike paced the office in agitation.

"He comes to work on my truck, he knows I'm Greek, and he's a Turk! What the hell did he think would happen when I found out?"

"I'm sorry I didn't know anything about his background, Mike," Rafer said.

"Turks have been butchering Greeks for hundreds of years, burning houses, raping women, and stealing children!"

"Jesus Chris', Mike!" Benny joined Mike's outrage. "I never knew not'in' 'bout that! You got a right to be mad!"

"I told the sonofabitch I wasn't going to call him S.K., that I was going to start using his real name, Suleiman! Everyone will know he's a goddam Turk!"

"Serve him right!" Benny cried.

Mike seemed aware suddenly that he was ranting.

"Hell, I know you guys aren't to blame," he made an effort to curb his wrath. "I burst in hollering about this Turk like he's number one on the FBI list. You both must think I'm nuts!"

"I don' t'ink you're nuts, Mike!" Benny said indignantly. "W'at them Turks done to your people, believe me, I'd be sore too!"

Mike looked at Rafer and frowned.

"I know what you must be thinking, Rafer," he said more quietly. "I've worked with guys of every nationality and color. You wonder why the hell I can't work with this Turk?"

"I understand, Mike," Rafer said. "Those old hatreds are hard to shake off."

Mike slumped wearily into a chair. For several moments, he sat scowling and silent.

"The truth is, I'm mad not only because he's a Turk but because the sonofabitch is a good iceman," Mike said grudgingly. "I mean, he's the best I've seen since Israel and Pacheco. He cuts and throws the ice like he was born to it."

"Earl saw him on your truck today," Rafer said. "He's taking him off."

"I figured Earl saw him," Mike shrugged. "I don't give a damn because we couldn't keep working together anyway."

"He's been getting good reports on him from the yardmasters," Rafer said. "He's giving S.K. his own truck."

"That figures, too," Mike said somberly. "Even Earl must know this guy's got the stuff to make a good iceman." He paused. "The Turk might just decide not to stick around. I really laid into him, raked him over the coals. He may be mad enough to quit."

He sat for a moment in silence.

"Truth is, he laid into me, as well," Mike said ruefully. "He kept quoting from the Bible to claim his people weren't the butchers I said they were." He stared down at his hands clenched into fists on his knees. "I suppose even a Turk has the right to be called anything he wants," he said slowly. "If he wants to go by S.K. because he's ashamed of who he is, that's his business."

"Getting his own truck will mean more money for him," Rafer said. "He may decide to stay."

"If he does stick around, I suppose I should give the sonofabitch a chance to show whether he's a stand-up guy, even if he's a Turk."

"That makes sense," Rafer said.

"But so help me, if he fucks up, then by God, it's Suleiman!"

Mike's voice grew heated again. "And I'll lean on the sonofabitch so hard, he'll be happy to quit!"

He rose and, with a curt nod to Rafer and Benny, walked briskly from the office toward the lockers.

"I never seen Mike so mad," Benny said. "I thought he was gonna kill bot' of us. Now he says he's gonna work with the Turk. How you figger that, Rafer?"

"Maybe S.K. being a good iceman is more important than his being a Turk," Rafer said.

"Well, it beats hell out of me." Benny slumped back in his chair.

The following morning, soon after Rafer arrived at work, Earl called S.K. into the office. Rafer wondered if the young Turk would reveal any anger or bitterness about his confrontation with Mike. But S.K. stood impassively waiting for the straw boss to speak.

"I'm giving you your own truck," Earl said. "Don't screw it up."

S.K. stared at Earl for a moment and nodded.

"There'll be more dough in it for you," Earl said. He looked at the schedule on his desk. "Take number 27. We'll put Link on as your helper. Now go get it loaded."

As S.K. started from the office, he paused at Rafer's desk.

"I want my name changed on the work schedule and payroll," he said, and there was a flinty edge to his voice. "From now on, use my first name. Suleiman."

"What the hell kind of a name is Suleiman?" Earl asked.

"It's Suleiman Khalid Nazim," S.K. bristled slightly. "I'm a Turk. Is that a problem?"

"I don't give a damn if you rode down on a jackass from Mars," Earl snapped. "Just do your goddam work."

Suleiman remained at the Team Track, but within a few days, the laggard Malvolo, who had been assigned to Mike, decided to quit. Rafer overheard him complaining to several men.

"That old iceman like to work me to death!" Malvolo said. "Every damn thing I was doing was wrong! Started bitching at me first thing in the morning and never stopped!"

To replace Malvolo, Earl assigned Trebek, another of the clumsier men, to Mike. At first Rafer thought the assignments were at random. He learned otherwise a week later. After Mike worked diligently to train the awkward helper, Earl switched men again.

Rafer made certain Mike knew that he had nothing to do with the assignments.

"I know that, Rafer," Mike grinned. "The fat man thinks he's screwing me, but all he's doing is giving me a chance to train the weakest guys here into becoming better icemen."

There was a day in that sweltering June when the heat seemed to reach its zenith. Cooler weather had been predicted, and as if to savage the city one last time, the temperature soared to 100. A half dozen trucks had overheated or broken down, and Earl had been tormented by a dozen calls from downtown. By the end of the day, his despair and frustration boiled over into rage. Rafer was gathering bills of lading in the locker room, crowded with men washing and changing, when Earl strode in from the office. The sight of him choked off the laughter, and men fell nervously silent.

"Downtown has been getting pounded all day by yardmasters' gripes!" Earl said harshly. "They're bitching to me about the lead-assed icemen I send to ice the cars! You think this is a goddam picnic? You're here to work! Any man don't work can turn in his time and get the hell out!"

Afterwards, he singled out individual icemen.

"Mitchell, you took an hour to clear the I.C.! Harrison, you took so goddam long to reload, you backed up two other trucks. Gevins, why didn't you report that breakdown sooner! By the time Salvatore got there, half your ice had melted!"

The men mumbled assorted excuses, delays in locating a car, a traffic accident, the engines overheating, their inability to get to a phone.

"Don't give me that crap! Your goddam job is to ice the cars! Ice them quick and then get to the next yard! If you can't do the work, then get the hell out!"

Even the veteran ice men weren't spared Earl's abuse. He lashed out at Sigmund and Thadeus for something he felt they'd done. While the two Polish icemen couldn't fully understand what he was saying, they were familiar with Earl's curses and listened stolidly to his tirade. When Earl paused for breath, Thadeus said something to Sigmund that sounded like "Fug'm!" Sigmund nodded somberly and then both men turned scornfully away.

Their contempt further inflamed Earl, but there was little he could do besides curse them. They were skillful, hard-working icemen who were familiar with every railroad yard in the city. Any effort to fire them would have dire consequences for Earl with the bosses downtown.

Earl also criticized Noodles, Stamps, and Mendoza.

"You should know better!" he ranted. "You take an hour to ice three cars, what the hell you expect new guys to do? You're supposed to set an example!"

Since their experience and ability protected their jobs, as well, the veterans had learned the most sensible response was to remain silent and ignore Earl's wrath. After the straw boss moved on, Noodles glared daggers at his back, Mendoza banged his locker door, while Stamps muttered curses.

The only iceman Earl never criticized before the others was Mike. A wary truce prevailed between them. Earl left Mike alone and Mike didn't challenge Earl when he berated the other workers.

At that moment, Suleiman entered from the yard, walking through the crowd of cowed, silent men to his locker. Earl watched him balefully and then moved toward him. The contrast between the two men standing side by side was startling. They were nearly the same height, but while Earl's bulk was ungainly and misshapen, Suleiman's body reflected symmetry and strength.

"When I gave you your truck, I thought you could do the job," Earl snarled. "You were at the Beltway an hour and a half today. Those two potato cars should have been done in twenty minutes."

"They switched the train, boss," Suleiman shrugged. "Yardmaster couldn't locate the cars."

"That's no goddam excuse! Don't let them pull that shit on you! Time means money!"

Suleiman looked contemptuously at Earl and turned to his locker.

"I'm talking to you!" Earl shouted. "Don't turn your goddam back on me!" He reached out and grabbed Suleiman's shoulder with his hamlike hand.

Suleiman whirled around and roughly shoved Earl's hand away. There was a sudden tensing of his body, a flare of rage in his face that forewarned violence. Rafer felt his breath constrict in his chest.

Mike was at his locker nearby.

"I was icing on another spur at the Beltway today while he was there," Mike said brusquely. "A brakeman switched the wrong train and screwed up the whole yard. There wasn't a thing anybody could do about the delay."

Earl looked shocked at Mike's violation of their truce.

"You're a hell of a guy to make excuses!"

"I'm not making excuses," Mike's voice rose. "Check with the Beltway yardmaster."

"You think I got nothing better to do than phone all over the city, checking out lies and excuses?"

"If you don't want to check, then quit your bitching," Mike said.

Earl's big body recoiled as if Mike had struck him.

"Who the hell are you, old man, to tell me what to do! You've been around too damn long, and everyone knows you can't cut it anymore! Other men are doing your work!"

Now it was Mike who seethed with outrage and anger.

"You lie in your goddam teeth!" Mike's voice carried like thunder through the room. His body trembled with a massive effort to control his fury. "Find one man in this room to say I'm not doing my job! Goddam you, liar that you are, find just one!"

Earl seemed to realize that his anger had driven him too far. He twisted around to stare desperately at the silent men, seeking one ally, one bootlicker, he could call upon for support. But Mike's prowess at icing was so well respected by the men that it would have been absurd for anyone to say otherwise. Earl knew what the response would be, and he turned and pushed his way roughly through the men, retreating in mute fury from the locker room.

Rafer, standing near the door, hurried to his desk a moment before Earl entered the office. The straw boss sat down, livid with frustration and rage. Rafer knew his humiliation before the men could only intensify his hatred of Mike.

In the last week of June, across the world from the U.S., a firestorm took place that overshadowed the small insular tensions and conflicts of the Team Track. The armies of North Korea crossed the 38th parallel and invaded South Korea. Within hours, President Truman declared war against North Korea as part of a United Nations peace action and ordered that U.S. troops be sent in to help the South Koreans resist the attack.

In the days that followed, whenever Rafer picked up a paper, large black headlines reported on the war. All the radio programs were interrupted by bulletins. There were also ominous warnings from the Soviet Union about the U.S. intervention. Rafer found it hard to believe that so close on the heels of one cataclysmic war, the world seemed primed for another conflict.

While the war depressed Rafer, it excited the young men at the Team Track. Andy, a lanky twenty-year-old from a small town in Georgia, gave notice he was quitting to join the army. He waved aside Rafer's suggestion that it might make sense for him to wait.

"I don't wanna miss out on this one too, Rafe!" Andy said earnestly. "My older brother was with the marines in the big one! When he came home, our town went nuts over him! The prettiest girls wanted to marry him! Mr. Slocum Page, who owns the bank, offered him a great job! I never thought I'd get my chance this soon! I'm going down right now to enlist!"

In a burst of patriotic fervor, a half dozen other young workers followed Andy and quit to enlist.

In the Team Track office, Earl carried on vehemently about the way he felt the war should be concluded.

"Drop the atom bomb on the bastards!" he said loudly to Rafer and Benny. "Quit fooling around and just wipe the bastards out!"

Rafer felt that using the atom bomb once again would cost

hundreds of thousands of innocent lives. But he said nothing about his feelings to Earl.

The war also caused him to reflect on his struggle to stay sober and return to his family. His own fate seemed trivial and insignificant beside the deaths of young soldiers and civilians in the bloody landscape of Korea.

Around the middle of July, the weather finally turned cooler. But the weeks of scorching heat had left the city as burned out as a landscape ravaged by fire. Nor could the cooler weather disperse the stale, scorched air still trapped inside rooms and buildings.

Back in his hotel after work, Rafer felt his room airless and stifling. He stripped off his sweat-soaked clothing and showered and dressed. Afterwards, in what had become the brightest part of his day, he walked downstairs to the room of the librarian, Leota, who had come several weeks earlier with Kelly from AA in response to his call.

A week earlier, on an impulse, he had knocked on her door. When Leota answered, Rafer, trying to sound casual so she wouldn't think he was coming on to her, asked if she'd like to have dinner. She agreed and they walked down to a nearby restaurant. Both of them enjoyed the evening.

Each night for the week that followed, after Leota returned from her job at the library and Rafer got back from the Team Track, they ate together. Rafer began looking forward to the evenings.

In their hours together, both spoke of their past. Rafer told Leota he'd been a teacher. He also told her of his drinking and his struggle to remain sober. For some reason not totally clear to him, he avoided telling her he was married or about his hope that someday he'd become worthy to return to his wife and daughter.

In fragments, he also learned about Leota's life. She came from a small town in Ohio, her father a storekeeper, her mother a housewife. She had three sisters, one of whom had died a year earlier.

She had told him on the first night they met how she'd started drinking as a cheerleader back in high school. During one of their evenings together, she expanded on that experience.

"You might not believe it to see me now," she said quietly, "but I was a good cheerleader. Not the best or the prettiest but still one of the team. I've told you how the girls partied with the football players, drinking and smoking grass. I didn't really enjoy it in the beginning, but after a few drinks, I felt prettier, felt that I really belonged with the pretty girls and the good-looking boys."

During the war, she attempted to enlist in the Women's Army Corps but was rejected because of a flawed disk in her back. She had been sober for a while, but that rejection started her drinking again.

"You know how it goes," she said. "I'd stop for a while. Then there'd be some disappointment, maybe an argument with my parents, and the way I kept from feeling miserable was to have a few drinks."

She spoke quietly, sparing herself nothing. He admired her honesty.

Leota also hinted at an unhappy love affair in her past, but she didn't elaborate. Finally, she told Rafer that in the fall, she planned to enroll in a city commercial college to study shorthand and typing.

"The library isn't a bad place to work," she said, "but five years from now I'll still be in the same job. I want to improve myself."

Little by little, these spare disclosures drew them closer. On one of their walks back to the hotel from the restaurant, Leota took Rafer's hand, her slim fingers moist and trembling in his palm. He suspected she was becoming fond of him. He was lonely and enjoyed her company, but her growing attachment made him uneasy, as well. Yet he remained silent about his family. He feared if she found out he was married, she might not want to go out with him anymore.

He also discovered Leota was very religious. She had been raised a Presbyterian, had drifted from the church, and then about five years earlier, had been returned to faith by an evangelist preacher named Blind Dobby during a revival meeting at the Pacific Garden Mission Church.

"I've always felt those evangelists were scam artists," Rafer said, "exploiting people for their money."

"That wasn't true for Pastor Dobby," Leota said. "He was the most inspiring human being I've ever heard. He's dead now, but I'll always be grateful to him for bringing me back to Jesus Christ."

She sensed the skepticism in his silence.

"It's hard for someone who hasn't experienced it to understand," she said earnestly. "You have to be in a group of unhappy, desperate people searching for hope and faith. Then, when a truly great preacher like Blind Dobby speaks, he reawakens your passion for Jesus. In that moment, your heart beating with all those other hurting hearts, sometimes miracles, like a woman rising from her wheelchair to walk, can truly happen."

Leota told him she still attended the Pacific Garden Mission Church, which was now served by a preacher named Israel. Rafer recalled Mike speaking of the preacher as having once been a great iceman.

"There's a prayer service this Sunday evening," Leota said. "I'd love for you to come with me."

"We'll see," Rafer said. He wasn't eager to join any assembly of zealots. He resolved that if she asked him again, he'd find some excuse not to go.

The following day, Saturday, fleeing the shabby, teeming neighborhood, Rafer and Leota drove east to the lake. They strolled hand in hand on the walk along the lakefront with a breeze off the water cooling their faces.

After a while, they paused to sit on a bench that looked across the sleek-hulled, white-sailed boats moored in the harbor.

"It's two different worlds," Leota said pensively. "The neighborhood where we live and work with its bars and tenements and then, just a few miles across the city, the elegant shops along Michigan Avenue and this lovely lakefront. Even the people look different, I mean, more like people look in movies." She leaned her head against his shoulder. "When I finish business school, maybe I can get a job in one of the offices downtown. I might find a place to live near here too." She smiled. "You could find a job around here too, perhaps begin to teach again in one of the city schools. We'd be able to spend weekends like this together."

That afternoon, while they lunched in a small Michigan Avenue café, she confided in him about her aborted love affair.

"I was working as a waitress then," she said. "He was a salesman for a restaurant supply house that sold my boss canned goods. He was good-looking with red hair and a smooth manner. I'm sure he charmed many other women the way he charmed me, but I was lonely, and I let myself believe he really loved me."

Her melancholy voice rose and fell against the murmur of voices around them.

"One day he just stopped coming into the restaurant," she said. "When I asked the salesman who took his place about Ralph, that was his name, the salesman said that he'd left the company. I waited for him to call or write but I never heard from him again. For weeks, every time I thought about him, I'd start to cry." She paused and gently squeezed his hand. "Since meeting you, Rafer, I don't think about him anymore."

As they drove back to the neighborhood that evening, Leota shifted closer to him in the car. Several times in the past when he had been attracted to a woman, Rafer had still remained faithful to his family. But he liked Leota more than any of the others, and that made him apprehensive. He vowed he'd tell her about Mellie and Rosie the first chance he could.

When they entered the hotel elevator, Rafer moved to press the button for Leota's floor so he could walk her to her door. She reached past him and pushed the button for his floor.

"I don't want this lovely day to end," Leota said. "Can we stay together a little longer?"

"That's fine," he subdued his uneasiness. As they left the elevator and walked down the corridor to his room, her thigh brushed his leg. He fumbled with his key, and when the door opened, they entered the small room.

He was grateful for the lemon and red glow of the signs from

Halsted Street, which softened the shabbiness of the walls, the faded lampshade, and the bed with its frayed spread. The street noises were also muted in the droning of the fan.

In the close, confining space, Rafer felt his body stirring with desire at the prospect of making love to Leota. He considered the words he'd say to begin, and then he was startled when Leota came quickly, urgently into his arms. Her slim-fleshed body emitted a scent of perspiration and a faint aroma of a flowered perfume. She raised her face to him, and he saw her eyes, misted and alluring, waiting for his kiss. His body responded with an urgency of its own, and he kissed her.

After the kiss ended, he felt clumsy and excited, as if he were a teenager about to have sex for the first time. She tugged her dress down off her shoulders, and the multicolored light gleamed across her naked throat. Her body seemed to flow toward his hands, and he fumbled to unhook her brassiere and freed her small, still-lovely breasts. He fondled them, feeling his fingers, barren for so long, suddenly tingling and alive. They sat on the edge of the bed, and he tugged up her skirt and stroked her thighs. He kissed her again.

When the long, intense kiss ended, she drew in a long, unsteady breath. She embraced him tightly, her cheek pressed against his shoulder.

"The wonder of it," she whispered, her voice trembling. "The wonder that after all these years I should find love once again. Oh, Rafer, God brought you to me."

He was stunned by her words. He hadn't thought of their relationship as love but as the desire of two lonely people. He was swept with remorse that cut him to the core and weakened his desire. He knew that every moment he waited, every caress and whispered endearment would make it harder to stop.

"Leota," he drew back. "Leota, listen . . . there's something I need to tell you . . ."

As if she sensed something dreadful about to happen, her hand fumbled to her throat, her arm shielded the nipple of one breast. He saw terror in her face.

"I have a wife and daughter," the words tumbled from his lips. "I left them a year ago so I could fight the drink on my own. I've been trying to stay sober, earn the right to go back to them. They're all I live for . . ."

For a moment, she didn't move, and he could almost hear her heartbeat. Then she swung gracelessly from the bed to her feet. The softness and warmth in her face seemed frozen into stone. She groped behind her for support, found the wall.

"Forgive me because I didn't tell you," he pleaded. "I was lonely . . . didn't want to lose your company. I'm so sorry, Leota . . ."

He braced himself for her anger, waited for the bitter words she might hurl at him.

But she didn't speak. She fumbled at her skirt, tugged her dress back over her shoulders, then fled from his room, her brassiere trailing from her hand.

Rafer sat there listening to the droning of the fan, his body alternating between sweat and chills. Had she cursed him, it might have provided both of them a kind of release. He considered going after her, to try to tell her once again how sorry he was. He decided it best to leave her alone for a while.

He passed the hours of that night sleepless and wretched. He saw the pale daylight replace the neon lights streaming in his window and heard trucks rumbling along Halsted Street. Barefooted and in his underwear, he walked wearily down the corridor to the bathroom.

When he returned to his room, he'd made up his mind to go to Leota. After he'd dressed and as he walked down the stairs to her room, he tried to think of what he would say. He knocked quietly on her door. There wasn't any answer. He thought she might be sleeping and he considered returning later, but he feared his resolve might falter. He knocked again, a little louder, still heard nothing. He turned to leave and then, on an impulse, quietly tried the knob. The door was unlocked, and when it opened, he was assailed by the sweet smell of cheap wine.

"Oh Jesus Christ!" he said in shock. "Jesus Christ!"

Inside the hot, windowless room, the stench of wine was suddenly overpowering. When his eyes grew used to the dark, he saw Leota's figure on the bed, partially covered by a sheet. He bent closer, saw her pale cheek, her hair tangled across the pillow, her mouth slack in heavy, drunken sleep.

He shivered and sat down at the foot of her bed. She stirred restlessly, mumbled a few words he couldn't understand, and then fell silent again. He felt as if he were witnessing the death of another human being.

He saw the glint of a wine bottle on the floor beside the bed and he picked it up. It wasn't yet empty, and without dwelling on Mellie and Rosie or all his anguished efforts to stay sober, he unscrewed the cap and raised the bottle to his lips. He took several deep swallows, emptied the bottle, the wine flowing like an elixir down his throat.

He marveled how easy the relapse had been. The shadow of the war, the tension of working with Earl, his endless struggle to keep from drinking all linked seamlessly in that instant with what he had done to Leota and brought the bottle to his lips.

He left her room, closing the door quietly. He walked down to a liquor store just opening on Halsted Street and bought two fifths of wine and a bag of chips. He returned to his room, and with as much excitement as he had anticipated making love, he started drinking again.

He'd consumed almost a full bottle before he began to feel drunk. It started with lightheadedness, his body weight seeming to vaporize, a certain buoyance in his limbs. His remorse slipped into euphoria when he felt everything might work out. He'd somehow make Leota understand. She might even forgive him because he had chosen a harder road by honoring his vow to his wife and daughter.

Then his reason failed, and the room filled with apparitions. He saw Mellie's sorrowing face, and he heard Rosie crying. He suddenly felt they were lost to him forever.

In the past, when things had seemed most hopeless, he'd considered suicide. Those furies returned to bedevil him now. He thought of ways to die, a gun to his head, a car in the garage with the motor running and a brick on the accelerator, a noose dangling from a beam. Thinking of ending his life violently brought on a nausea that surged up from his belly and burned his throat.

He fell back into a clammy sleep and woke with his throat parched. He struggled off the bed and opened the second bottle of wine.

After drinking half the bottle, he lay down again. He drifted in and out of sleep, a weird seesawing in which he lost track of time. When he woke again, the room was once more bathed in the lemon-red glow and he realized he had slept through the day. That eerie light brought back the specter of Leota with her small, forlorn breasts, her slip wrinkled about her waist, strands of hair matted to her cheek.

His sweat had chilled on his body and he shivered. He held the bedpost and pushed himself to his feet. The fever of his drunkenness had lessened, and he was stricken suddenly at the immensity of what he had done to Leota and to himself. All the months of their struggle to stay sober had been slashed to shreds.

He slipped into his robe, took razor, cream, and a towel and walked down the hall to the bathroom. He shaved slowly, his fingers trembling, and nicked himself several times. Afterwards, he showered and returned to his room to dress. When he looked at his face in the small mirror above his dresser, a strange, anguished countenance returned his gaze.

He walked upstairs once more and knocked on Leota's door, vowing to help her sober up. When there wasn't any answer, he tried the knob once more and entered the room. Leota's bed was empty. He reproached himself for not having come to her sooner.

He waited a while thinking she might have gone out for more wine. When she didn't return he feared she might be drinking in a bar on the street. Then he remembered she'd spoken about the Sunday evening prayer service at the Pacific Garden Mission Church. He might find her there.

He left the hotel and walked toward the church a few blocks away. Feeling suddenly weak, he stopped in a diner for a cup of black coffee. As he resumed walking, the rumble of passing trucks and cars beat like drums inside his throbbing head.

When he entered the gray-stone mission building, an old man directed him downstairs to a large basement room filled with rows of chairs. The room, which was cooler than the street, was partially filled with men and women, but he didn't see Leota among them.

The occupants were mainly street people, shabbily dressed, a few holding shopping bags on their knees. He was surprised to see about a dozen young icemen from the Team Track. Several saw him and waved weakly, and he waved back. He noted their hungover and besotted faces. Glutted by liquor and sex, perhaps they came to the mission church seeking absolution. They probably assumed he was there for the same reason.

Along the rear wall of the room was a long table with bottles of soft drinks, paper cups, and a platter of doughnuts. At the front of the room hung a large scarlet banner that read JESUS LOVES YOU. Below the banner, on a small platform, stood a wooden pulpit and beside it, a large, rough-hewn wooden cross such as early Christians might have fashioned in the days of Rome.

Rafer sat on an aisle chair near the middle of the room, so he could watch for Leota. He hoped fervently that she might still come.

A black woman in an ankle-length scarlet gown began the service by singing a hymn. Her voice resounded sweetly through the low-ceilinged room. Afterwards, she announced a number in the hymnal and the audience joined her in song. Across the aisle from Rafer, an old woman singing loudly glared at him in disapproval for his silence.

After the hymn, the preacher Rafer took to be Israel emerged from an alcove. He was a tall, granite-faced man, lean and weathered as a sun-scorched tree, with a shock of tangled white hair. He wore a dark collarless shirt and a dark jacket. When he raised his hands in greeting to the congregation, Rafer saw his deformed fingers. Taking his place at the pulpit, the preacher stared out across the gathering.

"Thank you all for coming to share our evening prayers," the preacher said, his voice resonant and clear. "It is through prayer that we relieve the hunger of each generation to renew its faith. Faith is eternal. Only our perishable bodies, only these are said to have an end."

His strong voice pierced the haze of several homeless men who had been slumped, half-asleep in their chairs. They raised their heads like startled deer, leaned forward to listen.

"Tonight, once again, we have some of the young icemen from the Team Track with us," the preacher said. "We are thankful to have them join us in the spirit of repentance, although"—a bemused smile lit his face—"we understand that next week they will exercise their free will to sin once more."

Several of the icemen shifted uncomfortably in their chairs.

"Tonight my sermon will address these young men," the preacher said gravely, "but what I say will bear relevance for all others who are here, as well. Indeed, relevance for all of us who are human."

His gaze returned to the young men.

"All you young stalwarts see of the ice you work with daily are common blocks that you score and cut," the preacher said. "But what appears to you as ordinary is truly extraordinary. Ice is colorless, odorless, tasteless, transparent. Think of it as a gem, a kind of diamond with magical properties. As the diamond when it turns in the light forms a prism of colors, so ice reflected in shades of light sparkles like a rainbow."

He raised one of his deformed hands to brush back his tangled white hair.

"Now it is also true that ice may be the most destructive force on earth," the preacher said. "As water falls below freezing, it takes up more and more space until, when it has frozen, it has greatly increased in volume. The power of this expansion is awesome, capable of shattering massive boulders, buckling the sturdiest of roads, cracking walls and foundations. I tell you, my brethren, beware of this force we call too simply, *ice*."

His words rang through the silence of the room, echoed from the corners, slowly faded.

"We know the earth began in fire," the preacher continued, "but over millions of years, our planet turned cold. Snow fell and the ice came, mighty glaciers that blew upon the earth the breath of a cataclysmic frost. Then, once again, in the fire of our sun, the earth was revived."

He paused, his voice suddenly somber.

"Fire and ice are the polarities of our galaxy," he said. "From the beginning of time, alternating epochs of heat and frost, the ancient, eternal struggle between these elemental forces continues."

An old man near the front of the room emitted a sibilant snore. The preacher looked down at him sternly. As if Israel had willed the prodigal awake, the old man's head snapped up.

"The great poet Dante understood the duality of fire and ice," the preacher said. "In his journey through the inferno, he described a place of enormous fires which, in level after level, scorch and sear the souls of evil men and women. Yet, in the very deepest level of hell, Dante tells us, a great wild-winged dragon lives, a creature flailing its massive wings so fast and with such force that the storm of wind it creates turns the fires of hell into ice."

Somewhere in the room, an old woman loosed a soft, hoarse sob. Close to her a man coughed. A chair scraped across the floor, the sound jarring in the silence.

"Now all these ages of frost and fire have been rehearsals for the ultimate end," the preacher said. "When the final chapter of our earth is written, it is the ice that will prevail. The ice will come after the sun's fire burns out, after that flaming stellar body becomes a celestial cadaver, a white dwarf lost in space among the cinders of burnt-out stars and the husks of dead planets."

The preacher lowered his head for a moment and then raised it again. A growing fervor stirred in his voice, which rose and fell in waves across the room.

"Without the sun's life-sustaining heat," the preacher said, "the earth will turn frigid, blizzards of snow and mountains of ice sweeping across the planet, fashioning huge glaciers that will eclipse anything man can imagine. As this awesome power overwhelms us, we will understand how subordinate are all the other natural calamities we have endured. Earthquakes, tornadoes, floods, and wars, all will be swept aside before this ultimate devastation."

Rafer felt himself caught in the vision the preacher conveyed of the dead sun and the ice as a relentless force.

"God help us when that day of judgement finally arrives," the preacher said, his voice gaining still more power. "In that time, through God's vengeance and retribution, the earth will be purged of its evil, not by fire but by ice!"

Rafer shivered. He accepted the preacher's prophecy as a deserving punishment for his own sins.

"When this age of the ice befalls us," the preacher went on, "and all mankind is in danger of extinction, then the only mortals who may help a few humans survive are those who have labored with the ice, who esteem the ice, who understand the power and magic of the ice! Through these warriors of the glaciers, by the grace of God, some of humanity and the earth, as we know it, may be salvaged!"

The preacher's sermon finished so abruptly, for several minutes, no one in the church moved. Then a few street people rose and shuffled toward the soft drinks and doughnuts. The icemen whispered to one another and rose to leave, as well. A few men and women straggled forward to cluster around the preacher, whose lofty figure loomed above them.

Rafer watched as people departed to make sure he hadn't missed Leota. Several somber-faced icemen nodded to him as they left. When the hall was nearly empty, Rafer walked up the stairs into the city night.

Back on Halsted Street, he thought of stopping in a few bars to look for Leota, but the stirring of thirst deep in his throat made him fear he'd start drinking again. Several times he paused and peered through a bar window for a glimpse of her.

In the hotel, Rafer went again to Leota's room, but she hadn't returned. He considered waiting for her but his body felt battered and exhausted, and he needed sleep. By morning perhaps she'd have returned, and he'd try to see her then.

He went to his room and stripped to his shorts. The lemon-red glow of the signs taunted him. He sat under the beam of the small lamp and began a letter to his family.

> My dearest Mellie and Rosie:
>
> I am writing this note to tell you both how much I love you and miss you. The weather is cooler but the rooms are still hot and that makes it hard to sleep. I think a lot about both of you. Don't worry about me because I am doing fine.

His hand faltered. He crumpled the paper and vowed he'd try again in the morning. He settled wearily into bed, shut off the lamp, and turned to the wall, yearning for a few hours of sleep unbroken by grievous dreams.

On the threshold of sleep, a final image stormed the circle of darkness. He saw the great, wild creature from the preacher's sermon, the huge, winged dragon that lived in the lowest level of the devil's domain. He felt it flailing its wings with such fierceness and power that the firestorms of hell itself were turned into ice.

8

Mike

AT THE BEGINNING OF AUGUST, SUMMER ENTERED a spell of temperate weather, the days mild, the evenings cooled by breezes sweeping across the city from the lake. Daylight lasted until almost eight, and after the sun disappeared behind the skyline of the downtown city, a scarlet and yellow twilight lingered in the night sky.

However brief the relief from the summer heat, it made Mike feel quick-footed and energetic. He worked on the cars with a buoyance he hadn't felt in a long time. Yet he understood that the real reason for his heart's ease was Dolores's agreeing to become his wife. Fearing she might change her mind, he suggested they marry as soon as possible.

"As it is, you're getting a fairly old guy now," he told her. "And every week that passes, I'm a week older. So let's get on with it."

Dolores agreed to move ahead, but she continued to voice concerns.

"Don't feel you have to do this, Mike," she said, as they drove to the license office in downtown Chicago. "I'll come live with you anyway. So be sure marriage is what you really want."

"Don't try to back out now," he said sternly. "You told me yes, and I'm not letting you go back on your word!"

"We're both crazy," Dolores sighed, "but you're crazier."

They made plans for the wedding to be held at the Pacific Mission Garden Church with Israel as the preacher. Mike hadn't set foot in a Greek Orthodox church in years and felt more at ease with his old friend performing the ceremony.

"If there's any kind of church service you'd rather have, in any kind of church," he told Dolores, "why, you just tell me. Anything you want is foursquare with me."

"The mission church is the only one I've attended in years," Dolores said. "Even that hasn't been regular, but it's fine with me."

Mike invited the veterans from the Team Track—Sigmund and Thadeus, Stamps, Noodles, and Mendoza. In addition, he asked Rafer and Benny. A young iceman filling in on the dispatcher's desk replaced Rafer for the afternoon.

Since Mendoza had worked as his partner the longest time, Mike asked him to be his best man. Mendoza was excited and pleased.

"I'm honored to stand up for you, Mike," he said earnestly. "Can I ask just what it is a best man has to do?"

"I'm not sure, but I don't think it's very much. I guess you hold the rings until Israel asks for them."

"I can handle that!" Mendoza said with a grin.

Although all the girls at the Olympia Club would have wished to attend, Dolores invited only Aunt Cora and two girls who were her oldest friends. She waved aside Mike's suggestion that she invite more of the girls from the Club.

"I don't want my wedding to become a whore's convention," she laughed. "Besides, your ladies of the evening are notoriously sentimental, and they'd all be bawling. Aunt Cora, Carmencita, and Madeline will supply enough tears."

She also gently rejected Mike's suggestion that she buy a white dress for the wedding.

"Every whore in the city would laugh herself to death if word got around I walked into any church wearing white," she protested. "On the other hand, even if all the respectable matrons feel I should wear scarlet, I have a light blue summer dress that will do fine."

For his own wedding garb, Mike pulled from the back of his closet a dark gray suit he hadn't worn in ten years. He was pleased that he could still fit into it, but when he first tried it on, the pungent smell of moth balls made his head spin. He had to hang the suit on his back porch for two days to air away the odor.

The Saturday morning of the wedding was a bright, clear day, and the small group gathered in the mission church made a colorful assembly.

Sigmund and Thadeus were clad in nearly identical beige suits that bulged and wrinkled over their burly bodies and shirts with stiff, high collars that resembled formal attire from the turn of the century. Stamps wore a suit of bold yellow and white suede shoes. Noodles was clad in a flashy maroon jacket and green trousers. Rafer was dressed more sedately in a gray jacket and dark trousers, and Benny wore a black-and-white checkered sports jacket that hung loosely on his skinny frame. Befitting his function as best man, Mendoza paid forty dollars for a splendid new white suit that fit his athletic body flawlessly.

"I don't mind spending the dough," he assured Mike. "This is the first and, maybe, the last time in my life anybody's going to ask me to be a best man. Besides, when the girls in the Pink Garden see this suit, they'll treat me special because they'll think I got an inheritance from a rich uncle in Mexico."

However colorful the attire of the men, they were clearly eclipsed by the women. Aunt Cora, her bearing queenlike and imposing, golden-haired Madeline, and the ample-bosomed Carmencita were dressed in a triad of brightly flowered and sequined silk dresses that shimmered and sparkled.

But to Mike, Dolores appeared the loveliest of all, wearing a glistening sky-blue dress with a trim of white lace at the collar, her fine, soft hair coiled into a bun, and in her hands, a small bridal bouquet.

The wedding guests sat in a cluster of chairs in the large mission hall, while Dolores, Mike, and Mendoza took their places in front, facing Israel. As Dolores had warned Mike, before the ceremony had even started, the silence in the hall was broken by the soft weeping of Aunt Cora and the girls.

Then Israel spoke.

"This is a day, God be praised, I thought I'd never see," the tall, white-haired preacher said gravely. "As Mike's pastor and as his friend, I'm delighted. He and I are comrades who have labored together on the HiLifts for a good part of our lives." He paused and smiled wryly. "And, because we are good friends, I've consented to perform the bare-bones ceremony for this union he's asked for. I'm disappointed because I wanted to provide Mike and his bride the full panoply of pomp and circumstance. Three deacons as ushers and the mission choir to sing the hymns." He sighed. "Mike has assured me that his wish is also favored by Dolores, so I'll oblige them and you'll all get on quickly to your celebration luncheon. Now permit me a small digression before I begin."

He looked somberly across the small gathering.

"On this day when we are assembled to celebrate a happy event," Israel said, "Let us first pray for those who are desolate and suffering today. I'm speaking about the young American and Korean soldiers in Korea, and the Korean people, all snared in this war that confirms, once again, man's inability to live in peace. I ask you to join me in a prayer for them and for a timely and equitable end to the conflict."

Israel bent his head for an instant. When he raised it again, a warm smile illuminated his cheeks.

"Now, to begin our wedding service today, I ask these two people before me whether they truly love one another and wish to be joined in marriage."

Standing stiffly before the preacher, Mike and Dolores answered "Yes" in unison. Mendoza added an emphatic "It's fine with me too!"

"Since the bride, groom, and best man are pledged to this union, we will proceed," Israel said. He turned to Mendoza. "Do you have the rings?"

"Yes sir, Preacher!" Mendoza grinned. "Right here!" He fumbled in his pocket and brought out the small velvet box Mike had given him before the ceremony. He looked proudly back at the guests as he removed the two small gold rings from the box.

"Dolores, place his ring on Mike's finger," Israel said, "and Mike, place her ring on Dolores's finger."

When the rings had been exchanged, Dolores looked down at her hand with moist eyes. Mike pressed her arm in reassurance. Both looked back to the preacher.

"Mike Zervakis, do you take this woman, Dolores Fielding, to be your lawfully wedded wife?"

"I do," Mike said.

"Dolores Fielding, do you take this man, Mike Zervakis, to be your lawfully wedded husband?"

"I do," Dolores said in a low, shaken voice.

"Then by the power vested in me by the Mission Evangelical Church and by the state of Illinois," Israel said, "I pronounce you man and wife."

A fresh cascade of tears burst noisily from Aunt Cora and the girls.

"Do you have anything you need to ask me, Preacher?" Mendoza frowned. "Seems to me a best man should do more than just hand over the rings."

"They know you can't handle any more than that," Noodles, sitting beside Stamps, laughed.

"You're not even part of the wedding party, so just shut your mouth," Mendoza snapped.

"Luis Mendoza," Israel said gravely. "Do you endorse the marriage of Mike and Dolores, support it wholeheartedly, and pledge to remain their staunch and loyal friend for as long as you live?"

"Yes sir!" Mendoza said earnestly. "You better know it! I do!"

"All right, Mike," Israel smiled. "It's official. Now you can kiss the bride."

For an instant, Mike found it hard to believe that his life had changed so quickly. In the space of a few minutes, all the years he had lived alone had come to an end. He'd found a companion to share his days and nights. If they were lucky, they'd remain together until the death of one or the other. Swept by gratitude, he leaned toward Dolores and sealed their union with a gentle kiss.

"What kind of kiss is that?" Noodles scoffed.

"That is one useless kiss," Stamps agreed gravely. "Must be the way Greeks kiss."

"You yahoos kiss your way and I'll kiss mine!" Mike laughed.

Mike had arranged a wedding luncheon at the Temple of Apollo, the most elegant Greek restaurant on Halsted Street. The full wedding party, except for Israel, who remained at the mission and would join them later, walked the two blocks from the church to the restaurant. The early afternoon sun glowing down upon the colorful entourage caused a sensation among the neighborhood people, who gaped as if they were witnessing a circus parade. A number of men they passed called cheerful greetings to Aunt Cora and the girls. As Carmencita and Madeline waved back gaily, Aunt Cora hissed a warning.

"We should have driven over," Mike heard her lament in a low voice to Dolores. "Half the men on the street have visited the club."

Inside the spacious and finely appointed Temple of Apollo, they were greeted by Nick Poulakakis, the owner, a bald-headed, stocky man dressed formally in a white shirt, dark tie, and dark suit. He warmly congratulated Mike and Dolores.

"Welcome, my friends," he said gravely. "It is an honor for me to have your wedding celebration here. As a gesture of respect for my fellow Cretan, Manolis, whose family comes from a village on our beloved island less than ten kilometers from my own village, I am contributing the wine to this repast!"

"That's generous of you, Nick," Mike said. "Thank you."

"Good for you, Nick!" Noodles cried. "From now on you'll get more of my business than you've gotten in the past."

Nick looked coldly at Noodles in a way that suggested he wasn't overly enthusiastic about that pledge.

"They're just finishing setting up your table in the alcove now," the owner said. "It will take just a moment longer."

As the wedding party waited, Mike pointed out a young girl sitting primly on a high stool beside the cash register a short distance away.

"That's Nick's daughter," Mike whispered to Dolores and Aunt Cora. "She just sits there taking checks and making change. Her name is Artemis . . . I think something a little longer . . . Artemi-si-a, that's it, Artemisia."

The girl was no more than twenty, slender bodied and raven haired. Her complexion was a rich blending of cream and olive, her eyes large and dark. She wore a modest gray cotton frock that complemented her aloof loveliness.

Aunt Cora nodded her approval.

"If that beauty worked in the Olympia, I'd double my gross."

"Nick watches over her like a battalion of guards," Mike said. "God help the poor devil who tries to come on to her, either by word or by trying to hold her hand. Nick has a long-barreled black gun back of the bar. He'd pull out that gun and the guy would be a goner!"

"You're kidding, Mike!" Madeline exclaimed. "I can't believe her father would shoot a man just for flirting with her!"

"You bet he would!" Mike grinned. "Now, I don't know if he's actually killed anyone yet, but he has chased half a dozen guys, including a few of our boys, at least a mile down Halsted Street, waving that big gun in the air."

"If that's the way he is, I'd as soon not have that girl in my club," Aunt Cora frowned. "Shooting up the place wouldn't be good for business."

The owner returned and led them to an alcove where a long table had been set with a fine, white cloth and glistening crystal and china.

"How lovely!" Dolores said, and Aunt Cora and the girls echoed her praise. Everyone sat down, and two smiling waitresses began serving them a lunch of golden roasted lamb, artichokes in a lemon sauce, and browned potatoes. There was a Greek salad overflowing with olives, white feta cheese, and spicy green peppers. True to his promise, the owner sent them an abundance of bottles of red and white wine. Everyone drank liberally except Rafer, who drank coke.

Some weeks earlier, Rafer had missed three days of work and had returned shaken and pale. He confessed later to Mike that he'd fallen off the wagon and, when he returned, had to endure a brutal tongue-lashing from Earl.

"First day he hired me, he asked if I were a drunk, and I said no," Rafer confided in Mike. "You can imagine how mad he was when I came in hungover. If it weren't summer and he needed me, he'd have fired me right then."

"Hang in there, Rafer," Mike had told him. "One lapse isn't the end of the fight."

"I've started on the wagon again," Rafer said. "That's all I can do . . . start again."

As the luncheon progressed and everyone drank freely, the girl's faces became flushed, and they teased and flirted with the men from the Team Track. Aunt Cora cautioned them several times about maintaining decorum until she too relaxed in a euphoric haze.

Among the women, only Dolores drank very little. When Mike tried to refill her wine glass, she covered it with her hand.

"I don't want to dull the memory of this day by drinking too much," she told him. "I want to remember every moment for as long as I live."

Mendoza was the first to stand and raise his glass in a toast, his cheeks crimson and his eyes bright from the wine.

"I've never been a best man before," he began emotionally.

"And you'll never be again!" Noodles cried. "Goofing up one wedding is bad enough!"

"He didn't goof up anything," Dolores said. "He was a wonderful best man."

"You hear that?" Mendoza glared at Noodles. He raised his glass again.

"As I was saying, I've never been a best man before, but it was an experience I'll never forget. Mike trusted me to do the job right, and I hope I didn't let him down. Now, Mike is not only my friend but also my teacher. All I learned about icing, I learned from him. If I ever get married, I'm going to ask him to be my best man. So now, with all my heart, I hope he and Dolores will be most happy . . . most happy."

"By God, Mendoza, I got to give it to you!" Noodles exclaimed. "That was a good toast!"

"Damn right!" Stamps agreed.

After everyone applauded Mendoza, Sigmund and Thadeus were the next to rise, their faces slightly distended from wine, as well. They raised their glasses and delivered loud toasts in Polish to the newly married couple. No one could understand what they were saying, but everyone applauded heartily.

Rafer rose and offered his best wishes.

"Before I started work at the Team Track," he said, his voice sober and clear, "I thought only the ancient Greeks had heroic men. But seeing Mike work, and the example he sets for others, I know now a modern Greek can be heroic too. So, here's to Mike, and his bride, Dolores."

"That's a damn fine toast too!" Noodles said.

"Rafe's been a teacher!" Benny said as he struggled to his feet. "T'ats how come he says smart t'ings lik' that." His wine glass shook in his hand.

"I can' say no'tin' good as Rafe—" He swayed slightly and then, overcome by emotion, wasn't able to continue.

"C'mon, Benny," Mendoza urged.

"Here's to Mike . . ." Benny said finally, his voice trembling.

"Here's to Mike an' . . . an' to Dolores . . ." He collapsed back in his chair.

"That a boy, Benny!" Noodles said.

Mike shifted uncomfortably under the barrage of praise.

"All these guys have drunk too much," he muttered to Dolores.

"That's true," she whispered. "But they also care for you and respect you."

"The damn truth is, I've drunk too much too," he sighed, his head spinning as he rose to go to the washroom. "That's what happens when you're getting booze for free."

He started from the alcove and walked unsteadily through the restaurant. As he passed an adjoining room that held the bar, he glanced in and was startled to see the long-haired, towering figure of Suleiman sitting on one of the stools.

Mike stopped abruptly and stared, wondering whether the Turk was really there or an apparition come to cast a shadow over his marriage. When he realized it was really Suleiman, his heartbeat quickened at the coincidence of having the Turk in the restaurant on his wedding day. In an effort to collect his wine-fleeced senses, he fled to the washroom.

Mike had seen Suleiman at work and in the locker room but hadn't spoken to him since the day he'd learned he was a Turk. The following morning, Mike heard from Rafer that Earl had pulled the Turk off his truck. He also learned that Suleiman wanted his name used instead of his initials. Mike knew he'd taunted the Turk into making that change.

The sight of Suleiman also made Mike recall his confrontation with Earl in the locker room, when he had come to the Turk's defense. He had witnessed Earl abusing men and distorting the truth before and had never interfered.

But Mike had spoken out that night because the Turk was ready to assault Earl. Every man in the room would have cheered an attack, but Suleiman would surely have been fired. And the bewildering truth was that Mike didn't want the man fired.

All that had happened since then confirmed he had made the right decision. Suleiman's icing prowess was becoming renowned across the city. There were yardmasters who asked for him, several even needling Mike by telling him the Turk was his equal at the icing. That comparison didn't distress Mike but strengthened his conviction that Suleiman could become a great iceman.

When he had talked with the other veterans, Noodles and Stamps agreed.

"I swear, Mike, the guy can do things on the cars that I've only seen you do," Noodles said. "You'd think he'd been icing for years instead of a few months."

"He's one hell of an iceman, all right," Stamps said somberly, "but he don't know how to work with others. I seen guys like him in the army. They're outlaws, loners, who don't give a damn whether they make friends or not."

"He struts up on the cars like he's God's chosen iceman and tries to make everyone else look bad," Mendoza said grimly. "What I'd really like to do is shove my pike pole up his ass."

By the time he left the washroom, Mike had convinced himself that Suleiman's showing up in the restaurant on his wedding day was a good omen. At a time when Mike's hostility was tempered by his own happiness, he felt an urgency to make peace with the Turk.

He walked resolutely to the bar. At the last minute, wary about how the Turk might respond, he braced for rejection then tapped the young man lightly on the shoulder. Suleiman twisted around, his face revealing his surprise. Mike gestured casually toward the empty stool beside him.

"Okay if I join you?"

"I don't own the bar," Suleiman said. His voice wasn't friendly but neither was he hostile.

Mike sat down and ordered a shot of Jack Daniel's.

"You know you're in a Greek restaurant?"

"I know," Suleiman said, "but it's the only place in the neighborhood where I can get good Anatolian kebob." He paused, the smirk Mike resented reappearing on his face. "How about you? Didn't I hear you say to hell with Greek restaurants?"

"I meant to hell with owning or working in them. I don't have any problem eating in them. Besides, I got married today."

Suleiman stared at him in disbelief.

"You're probably wondering who the hell would want to marry an old bull like me, but it's true," Mike said somberly. "We're having a wedding luncheon in the next room."

"Well, all right," Suleiman tipped his glass. "People get married all the time. I guess I should say congratulations."

"Thanks."

They lapsed once more into silence.

"About that day on the truck," Mike said. "For thirty years, I've worked with guys of every nationality and background. There wasn't any reason we couldn't work together. I had no right to blow up."

Suleiman continued staring at his glass.

"And about your name," Mike went on. "Hell, what you want to call yourself is none of my damn business."

"I should have used Suleiman from the beginning," Suleiman said brusquely.

"Well, it still wasn't my business."

For an instant Suleiman looked sharply at Mike and then turned away.

"How about coming over a minute to meet my new missus," Mike said. "A few of the guys from the Team Track are there, and you can say hello to them too."

"Did you invite Earl?"

The question made Mike laugh. A trace of a smile curled around Suleiman's mouth.

"Hell no! Come on over."

"I don't want to butt in. Maybe they'll think a Turk isn't welcome at a Greek wedding."

"It's not a Greek wedding, just a wedding," Mike said. "And you won't be butting in. I got to tell you, the guys are drunk and probably won't remember you came over anyway."

Suleiman swung off his stool, and they walked together toward the alcove.

When they reached the table, the Team Track workers appeared surprised and then greeted Suleiman heartily. As if recalling how Mike had raged against the Turk in the office, Benny looked shocked at his presence. Mendoza stared reproachfully at Mike as if he'd been guilty of bringing in an intruder.

"This here's Suleiman," Mike introduced him to Dolores, Aunt Cora, and the girls. "We work together at the Team Track. He's got talent . . . I mean he's a real good iceman."

"Congratulations, Mrs. Mike," Suleiman said gravely to Dolores. "I hope your life will be happy and healthy."

"Thank you," Dolores said. "Won't you have a glass of wine with us?"

"I'm sorry, but I've got to go . . ." Suleiman said. "I've got people to meet." With a brisk wave to the gathering, he left.

"I don't believe what I just saw!" Noodles said. "Mike inviting a Turk to have a drink at his wedding!"

"I think marriage has changed the Greek already," Stamps said somberly.

"He wasn't invited," Mendoza said. "He had no business here."

"It's my wedding day and I asked him to come over," Mike said genially. "Trouble with you guys is, you're forgetting this is America! Even if Suleiman is a Turk, he's got some good qualities."

Carmencita and Madeline emitted heartfelt sighs.

"I don't think I've ever seen so big and so handsome a man," Carmencita said.

"I love his long, black hair!" Madeline said. "He reminds me of that character in the comic strips . . . you know . . . Prince Valiant."

"He is a magnificent-looking man!" Aunt Cora agreed. "Put a crown on his head and he could be a king."

"The icemen already have a king, and that's Mike," Mendoza said.

"Well, whatever the hell I am, I can't go on forever," Mike said impatiently.

"Does there have to be a king?" Dolores asked.

"There has to be someone, some kind of icemaster," Mike said earnestly. "Like Israel and Pacheco who were great icemen and then I came and learned from them." An urgency came into his voice. "And, after me, there needs to be someone who'll pass that skill on to the young guys who come later."

He became conscious of Dolores and the others watching him.

"Okay, okay, enough preaching!" he said, "Wait until you taste some of Nick's great Greek desserts."

"Hey, Mike," Noodles said. "Where are you and Dolores going on your honeymoon?"

"We can't go anywhere until the summer icing is over," Mike said. "In October, maybe we'll take a trip east. Dolores wants to see Niagara Falls."

"I was there once," Noodles said. "It's just a lot of water."

"Lots of lovers and newlyweds go there, Noodles," Mendoza said scornfully. "You got to be romantic to understand."

"You saying I'm not romantic?"

"You're a Casanova, but you're not romantic!"

Noodles appealed to Mike.

"Don't get me mixed up in your arguments," Mike said. "I got enough trouble trying to be romantic myself."

"Well, anyway," Noodles said. "I still say it's just a lot of water."

"I think they should go to Paris," Carmencita said pensively. "If I ever get married, Paris is where I would love to go."

Getting his apartment ready for Dolores, Mike had hired a pair of sturdy Bohemian cleaning women, who scoured the bathroom, washed the curtains and old tablecloth, and polished the furniture. In spite of these preparations, the first time Dolores entered, he was conscious of the apartment's cramped size and its shabbiness. He hadn't minded those conditions himself, but he was ashamed at having her see the way he lived.

"This is your home, and it will be my home too," she reassured him. "Don't worry about it. I have a few old family pieces of my own that Aunt Cora has stored for me and that I'd given up hope I would ever use. I'll bring them in, and pretty soon, you may not even recognize the place."

One of the first things she did was ask Mike to call her by her birth name, Reba.

"Dolores was my whorehouse name," she said quietly. "I made up my mind to use it for the last time when we were married. Now I know Reba isn't much of a name, but its who I am."

"I don't have a problem with that," Mike said. "Dolores or Reba, Queenie or Countess, you're my lady."

They began a ritual in the evenings when Mike came home from work. Reba ran warm water into the old tub. To make it hotter, she boiled several kettles of water. Mike stripped and lowered his body gingerly into the water. Reba knelt beside the tub, and slowly, she sponged his face and his shoulders, his back and arms. He'd recline in the tub and raise one leg, and she'd sweep the washcloth from his toes to his thighs. By the time she'd finished, the knots and soreness in his body had miraculously relaxed, his muscles and joints released from some of their tension and aches.

He'd rise dripping from the water.

"Coming out of the water, you look like one of those Greek gods," Reba told Mike once.

"You be careful now," Mike laughed. "Remember, those Greek gods were always horny as hell."

Reba would rub his shoulders and back briskly with a towel until he was dry. He'd slip into his old faded robe, which was ripped in several places (she vowed to buy him a new one), and they'd sit down to eat a green salad and a piece of beef or pork that Reba had prepared. She was apologetic about her cooking.

"You know, men didn't come to the Olympia Club expecting a gourmet meal," she said wistfully. "I didn't have much time to learn to cook."

But after years of opening cans and making bologna and cheese sandwiches, Mike found Reba's meals appetizing. He also enjoyed her companionship. Instead of eating in solitary silence, he had someone with whom to talk and laugh.

A transformation in Reba took place after she came to live with him. Freed from her need to primp and gild herself, her face devoid of any makeup, she appeared to him to have suddenly grown older. He became aware of tiny wrinkles at the corners of her mouth and around her throat, a shadow of aging under her eyes. He was surprised how swiftly those signs became visible, as if once she'd been removed from the spurious glitter of the brothel, she reverted to her real age. But none of these small marks of her aging bothered him because he still found Reba a beautiful woman.

Later in the evening, they'd go to bed naked using only a sheet to cover them. The old, worn mattress that had harbored his body alone for so long creaked as they moved close together. He lay on his side and, in the glow of the lamp, looked with pleasure at his wife's body. There were drops of sweat glistening on the fine down of her cheeks and throat. Her lovely breasts had fine veins and firm nipples. When she stretched her leg alongside his own, he felt her flesh, moist and warm.

Sometimes he couldn't resist reaching to fondle her, not driven by desire but by the delight he found in touching her smooth flesh. On a few occasions, his fondling escalated to lovemaking, but he had the uneasy feeling that she responded only to please him. Most of the time, they were content just to lie close to one another.

On those nights when the heat made it hard for them to fall asleep, the street noises muted by the droning of the window fan, Reba spoke of her past.

She had been an orphan, adopted when she was six by a childless, middled-aged husband and wife. A year later, the husband suffered a stroke that confined him to a wheelchair. All through her childhood, Reba recalled the wheelchair dominating and restricting life in the house. During her years in elementary school, she envied her schoolmates their freedom because she had to go directly home after school to help her foster parents.

When she began high school, a new world opened for her. She began to date in her freshman and sophomore years. In her junior year, she began staying out all night, and by her senior year, she was running wild. Her foster mother, beset by the problems of caring for her invalid husband, did little to discipline or restrain her.

"I slept with a few boys," Reba said. "No other reason than I liked a good time. I had a couple boyfriends but nothing serious, and I moved from boy to boy. The summer after I graduated from high school, a girlfriend took me to a party. There were older men at the party, and another girl told us they were wealthy businessmen who would pay generously to have sex with us. Since we'd been having sex for our own pleasure, it wasn't much different, and afterwards we were many dollars richer. Up to that time, I had never considered that I might get paid for doing what I enjoyed doing anyway. I guess that was the beginning."

She paused and sighed.

"I have to confess that my transition to becoming a whore was easy. Another girl told me about a house that catered to lawyers and doctors. She introduced me to the house mother, we called her 'Madam' then, and she hired me on the spot. I was young and good-looking with a wickedly alluring figure—don't look at the way I am now—and I became a favorite. Men asked for me, and while I never really loved any of them, they made me feel alive, made me feel that I was a woman able to make men happy."

She moved closer to him, her fingers gently caressing his shoulder.

"If this sad whore's tale bothers you, Mike," she said softly, "tell me to shut my big mouth."

"I've been going to brothels most of my life," Mike said, "and I never knew anything about the girls. Go on . . ."

The truth was, he enjoyed the sound of her voice. It was expressive, with quick liltings and, from time to time, a soft laugh that echoed pleasingly in his ears.

"As the years passed, any pleasure I felt began to fade," Reba said. "So did pride in myself as a woman. I began to feel used and tired. I would have been a poor whore if I hadn't made the johns feel they were special. But no matter what words I spoke or what sounds I made, I felt this weariness growing. That started to worry me, and I had to work harder and harder at showing pleasure when I felt nothing."

From one of the apartments beside their own, a man's hoarse voice rose in anger. There was the sound of a bottle shattering.

"That's Gorsuch slapping his wife around again," Mike said somberly. "I'll have another talk with the sonofabitch."

After a moment, the noises ebbed once again into the droning of the fan.

"A time came when fewer men wanted to take me to bed," Reba said, her voice grown pensive. "I couldn't blame them when there were so many younger girls instead. But I always kept some steady johns who had grown comfortable with me, men who wanted to talk." She laughed. "Would you believe, many nights I spent most of my time listening and talking?"

"Sure, I'd believe it," Mike said. "You're a good talker."

"Are you making fun of me?"

"Not me!"

"I talk so much because you talk so little!"

"I like it that way," Mike said. "Besides, I know those guys liked to talk to you because you've got a sensitive heart."

"Sometimes a whore's heart means a shriveled heart without any feeling left for anything or anybody," Reba said. "But sometimes, because of all she's heard and done, and the frailties she sees in people, a whore's heart can also be compassionate."

Her voice became sleepier.

"The truth is, I never heard a whore's story that had a happy ending," she said softly. "And I didn't think mine would be any different. I thought I'd just keep going, maybe end up in some crib where they never change the sheets, humping some human wreck for a dollar." She twisted closer to him, her breath warm and moist against his cheek. "Honest to God, Mike, it's a true miracle, ending up with a good man, a caring man. I'm grateful . . . truly grateful."

In the clasp of the summer night, his new wife beside him, Mike was also grateful. At this point in his life, to have found someone he loved who loved him was a treasure he had not expected. Reba was right in calling it a miracle.

9

Mike

IN LATE AUGUST, HEAT ONCE AGAIN RETURNED to the city, and the humidity rose, as well. Under the blazing sun, the streets and sidewalks smelled of burnt asphalt and brick. A hot wind blew from the south, whipping shreds of garbage and fragments of newspaper along the gutters.

While the heat earlier in the summer had drained Mike's energy, this new spell didn't seem to affect him, and he continued working with vigor. He felt his sense of well-being had come now that he had Reba and because he and Suleiman had put their quarrels to rest.

Mike believed the longer Suleiman worked with the ice, the greater the chance it might exert its magic upon him and he'd want to remain. The praise he heard about the young Turk from the yardmasters reinforced his hope.

"That big, long-haired kid is not only strong but quicker icing a car than anybody I've seen in a long time," a grizzled yardmaster Mike had known for many years told him. "Seeing him up on the cars reminds me of Israel."

On several occasions, unable to resist the excitement of watching him at work, Mike followed Suleiman to the yards. When Billy, the young helper on Mike's truck, asked what they were doing in the yard when there wasn't a car to be iced, Mike told him brusquely that it was none of his business.

There was a morning when Mike and Suleiman were both icing in the I.C. yards. As soon as he and Billy finished their cars, Mike drove to the nearby spur where Suleiman was icing. He parked a short distance away, and as he climbed down from the truck, on top of the car, he saw Suleiman's tall figure framed against the sky.

With the young iceman unaware of his presence, for several minutes Mike watched him at work. Suleiman had improved greatly since the week they had been together. His steps from truck to car platform were swift and surefooted, and he cut and threw the ice swiftly and with ease.

Suleiman finished the bunker and closed the plug. As he started walking to the other end of the car, he noticed Mike.

"Come to check up on me?" he called down.

"Hell, no!" Mike said. "Billy and me just finished on the north spur. Our ice is going to melt on the drive back, and I thought you might be able to use it."

"I got enough for this car," Suleiman said.

As his helper, Link, pulled their truck alongside the car, Suleiman crossed the platform and, with his tongs, clasped and swiftly dragged a four-hundred-pound block to the bunkers. He held the block upended for an instant and then, with a quick twisting motion, released the tongs. The block fell and split evenly, one half falling into one bunker and the second half jumping the edge to drop into the second bunker.

Link, standing on the truck elevator, shook his head.

"I still can't figure how the hell he does that," he said.

Suleiman gestured at Mike.

"Number one iceman down there taught me.," He grinned and spoke to Mike. "Look all right to you?"

"Not bad," Mike nodded gravely. "Not bad at all." He waved and turned away. "See you guys later."

As they drove from the siding, Billy, sitting beside Mike in the cab, spoke.

"Could you teach me how to split the blocks and drop them into the bunkers the way Suleiman was doing, Mike?" Billy said.

"I sure would like to learn how to do it."

"Sure, Billy," Mike sighed. "Keep from stabbing yourself with your pike pole long enough, I'll be glad to teach you."

In the locker room that night, Mike spoke about Suleiman to Noodles and Stamps.

"When you get a chance, one of you guys tell him that sometimes he hooks his tongs on the blocks too far away from the score marks," Mike said. "It's not a big deal, but if he makes the adjustment, it'll save him a few steps, a few swings."

A few days later, after a visit to the Indiana Harbor Belt Railway yard, where he observed Suleiman at work again, Mike made another suggestion to the veterans.

"When he's lifting the blocks, sometimes he doesn't bend his knees enough," Mike said. "That's putting tremendous pressure on his back. He doesn't feel it yet because he's so damn strong. But it's a bad habit for a man to get into."

"Hell, Mike, you're making good suggestions," Stamps said. "Why don't you tell him yourself?"

"I tried to hammer years of icing savvy into the guy in a single week," Mike said ruefully. "I don't want him thinking I'm hounding him again. It's better if you guys drop the hints."

Mike also carried his enthusiasm about Suleiman to Israel, over coffee one Saturday afternoon in the Santorini Bar.

"You got to see this young guy at work, Israel!" Mike said. "You remember Mandovich, that scabby old engineer at the Rock Island who's been around since the creation? He told me last week Suleiman is better now than I ever was!"

"Does that bother you?"

"Hell no!" Mike said emphatically "The better iceman he becomes, the better I like it!"

"You display the pride of a father longing for his son to surpass him," Israel said quietly. "And you may be right. Perhaps destiny has brought this young Titan along now, when you're close to leaving the HiLifts yourself. It has a Biblical significance, a reaffirmation of the cycle of life, death, and rebirth."

"You know better about what comes from the Bible than me,

Israel," Mike said. "But I'm more excited about this guy than I've ever been about any of the others I felt showed promise. Hell, Israel, I know I can't go on forever. Tell you the truth, now that I got Reba, and if this young Turk sticks around, I wouldn't mind putting my tongs and pike pole into storage."

"How does he feel about the icing?"

"He says icing isn't what he wants to do," Mike said somberly. "But, I tell you, Israel, he does it so well, it's hard for me to believe he'll really give it up!"

"We all come onto this earth seeking our place in the drama," Israel said. "You and I were fortunate we found it. But we can't choose for someone else. This man's fate may lead him in a different direction."

"I know he might leave," Mike said. "That's why I got to make him understand how the icing can be an adventure for him too. At the same time, I got to be careful I don't push him too hard."

"His staying or leaving may not rest in your hands alone," Israel said. "Don't forget that disciple of Lucifer in the Team Track office. We want this Turkish Achilles to remain, but perhaps Earl understands the danger Suleiman poses to his power. He'll do everything he can to get rid of him."

"I know he'd like to give him the boot!" Mike said grimly. "But if Earl did try to cut him loose, by God, I'll get every yardmaster in the city to raise a howl they'll hear in the offices downtown." He finished his coffee and rose to leave. "I got to go, Israel," he said. "I'm meeting Reba at the Athens Grocery. First time in twenty years she's got me buying food that doesn't come out of a can."

As Mike started away from the table, Israel called him back.

"Remember, old friend," Israel said quietly, there's human, wrist-watch time, and then there is God's time, the time of mountains and rivers. If this young Turk isn't the one to redeem us, the Lord won't abandon us. I believe he'll send us another redeemer someday."

"You're closer to God than I am, Israel," Mike said. "But if God's going to send us an iceman, I'd sure like to see him in my lifetime." He waved the old preacher good-bye.

At the Team Track, during that resurgence of summer heat, the great, sweat-drenched figure of the straw boss loomed once again on the hill, shouting at the drivers to reload quickly and keep the trucks rolling. Rafer told Mike there were also interludes when Earl sat silent and brooding at his desk. "I haven't any idea what he's thinking about," Rafer said, "but he has the look of a man in a dark depression. Sometimes he doesn't even seem to hear the phone."

When Mike had reason to enter the office, he didn't find Earl gloomy or distracted. All the man's energy and hostility seemed suddenly focused, and the exchanges between them were laced with bile. He knew Earl still seethed at the humiliation he had suffered in the locker room when Mike challenged him. And he knew the straw boss wouldn't rest until he had found a way to make Mike pay.

The heat continued into the beginning of September, the air itself on fire, the hot sun making the cab of the truck an oven. Mike's earlier vigor and euphoria drained away with his sweat. No matter all the reasons he had to feel good—the long, hot summer was burning him out.

His day began early in the morning with the first transfer of ice from the big house to the truck. He and Billy drove to the yards, iced the cars, and returned to the Team Track several times to reload.

By late afternoon, his exhaustion became an adversary, adding weight to his arms and legs, increasing pain in his neck and back. But he drove himself mercilessly, refusing to give in to any weakness until the day's work was done.

An affliction he had never experienced before rose to trouble him—brief, frightening spells of dizziness when the sky and earth seemed caught in a whirlwind. On one occasion, the dizziness struck him while he was driving, and with a flare of panic, he had to pull his truck quickly to the side of the street to get his bearings.

He considered seeing a doctor, but he'd been in robust health for so many years and had never needed a sawbones. He didn't favor the idea of seeking one out now.

Meanwhile, the war in Korea that had started in June continued, the daily newspapers reporting on the fighting, which grew more intense. The radio programs Mike and Reba listened to in the evening were interspersed with bulletins about military advances across villages with strange names.

The contradictory reports made it difficult to know which side was winning. One day the U.S. Air Force destroyed a contingent of North Korean tanks and troops. On the following day, North Korean tanks and troops inflicted heavy casualties on U.S. forces.

At the Team Track, each week saw one or two more of the young men quitting to join the army. Others planned to enlist as soon as the summer was over. Mike anxiously watched them go because he knew his son, Lucas, was about the same age as many of them. He felt a surge of fear when he considered his son might already be in Korea.

On those days when a railroad had a train of cars with dry bunkers needing seven or eight thousand pounds apiece to be iced, several trucks were dispatched from the Team Track to the same location. That occurred one morning when Mike, Mendoza, and Suleiman drove their trucks to ice a long train at the Rock Island and Pacific.

Mendoza and Suleiman and their helpers iced a string of fruit cars near the middle of the train while Mike and Billy iced a row of vegetable cars near the end.

For the fourth time in less than an hour, Mike corrected the way Billy swung his pole.

"I've told you over and over again!" Mike said in exasperation, "keep swinging wild like that, Billy, and you'll sure as hell stab yourself! You'll need your sorry ass carried into the Pink Garden!"

"I'm sorry, Mike," Billy said dolefully. "I aim the damn pole one way, but it just goes another."

When Mike looked down the track at the other crews, he saw Mendoza and Suleiman's trucks being driven slowly alongside the train. Balanced atop the platforms of the moving trucks were two figures he recognized as Suleiman and Mendoza heaving chunks of ice from the truck into the open bunkers of the cars.

Mike let loose a bellow of aggravation that was lost in the banging of freight cars nearby. He brusquely motioned Billy out of the way as he swung up into the cab and quickly drove the short distance to the other trucks. He brought his truck to a rubber-screeching stop alongside the one driven by Mendoza's helper, Gabe, who brought his truck to a stop. The other truck, driven by Link, also stopped. Mike jumped down from his cab.

"What the hell you guys think you're doing!" he shouted at Suleiman and Mendoza straddling the truck platforms. "A rut in the roadway or braking quick could send you flying! Get the hell down!"

Suleiman and Mendoza climbed down and swung off the trucks. Mendoza gestured sheepishly.

"We were just fooling around, Mike," he said. "I mean, I was showing the guy how to ice from a moving truck."

"Showing me?" Suleiman taunted him. "You can't show me a damn thing I can't do better!"

Mendoza's face flushed with anger, and he took a threatening step toward the bigger man. Mike stepped forward quickly to block his path.

"You only ice from a moving truck when there are empty bunkers on a train that's late to pull out," his voice trembled with an effort to control his anger. "It's not a game you play to see who can break his goddam neck first!"

Mendoza looked sullenly at the ground while Suleiman stared defiantly at Mike. He seemed about to say something, and then he shrugged and turned away.

That evening at the Team Track, Mendoza, Stamps, and Noodles came to Mike's locker.

"Listen, Mike, I know what I did today pissed you off," Mendoza said bitterly. "But you got to understand how I feel. You taught me how to ice, and you know I'm a damn good iceman. Now what gives this smart-ass the right to come in and try to show me up!"

"Maybe Mendoza shouldn't have been fooling around," Noodles frowned, "but you can understand him getting mad. This guy's brass riles all of us."

"Like I said before," Stamps said gravely, "the man is an outlaw, a loner. Guy like that makes trouble."

"All three of you are near the best damn icemen ever worked the HiLifts," Mike said earnestly. "At the same time, I got to tell you in thirty years, I never seen anyone take to icing so quick as this guy. I don't want to give up on him."

Mendoza started to interrupt, and Mike cut him off.

"Maybe he hasn't learned our ways yet," Mike said. "He hasn't learned to respect the work other men do. But I'm asking you guys, specially you Mendoza, as a favor to me, give him a chance. I swear I'll have a talk with him myself, make him understand he has to be part of the team."

Noodles and Stamps nodded their assent. Mike looked at Mendoza.

"All right, Mike," Mendoza muttered finally. "The sonofabitch burns me up, but if you talk to him . . . I'll back off for you."

The following evening, as Mike changed slowly in the locker room, he kept a watchful eye on Suleiman. Stalling for time, he lingered near the door while speaking casually to several men. When he saw Suleiman ready to leave, Mike left quickly and waited for him outside.

The first colors of the setting sun covered the shabby buildings of the Team Track with a scarlet glow. The darker shades of twilight concealed the crest of the hill and the row of trucks.

Suleiman came out of the locker room. He paused when he saw Mike.

"Got a minute?" Mike asked.

Suleiman waited.

"Yesterday at the Rock island," Mike said. "I'm sorry I yelled at you guys that way."

"You were worried about one of your boys."

"I was worried about both of you," Mike said. "Icing that way is too damn dangerous to do just fooling around."

"You do it, don't you?"

"I do only when it needs to be done."

"Does that mean no one else has a right to do it?" Suleiman said sharply. "Maybe the number one iceman is worried about others moving into his turf?"

"I'm not worried about that," Mike said quietly. "I'm just damn surprised you can do it after you been here so short a time. Mendoza may be the best iceman here, and it took him years to learn how to do what you did yesterday. That proves you're already a hell of an iceman . . . better than I am now because you're younger and quicker."

Suleiman seemed startled by the praise. He stared at Mike for a moment in silence and then shook his head.

"I'll never be good as you," he shrugged. "Maybe I can do the things you do, but you got something I don't have. Not that I give a damn. Like I told you before, if I got to name ten things I want to do, icing wouldn't be at the top of the list."

"Is it still at the bottom?"

Suleiman laughed.

"You're one Greek bulldog," he said. "You just don't give up, do you? Well, maybe it's not at the bottom. I got days heaving the ice when the work flows through me like a strong drink. But I got to tell you, it's still not number one."

"Things can change!" Mike said earnestly. "If you didn't have the heart for it, you couldn't do it so well!" He paused. "There's something else I been waiting to tell you . . . all that stuff I said about Turks . . . well, you've changed my mind. I mean, I'm a Greek and you're a Turk, but that doesn't matter anymore."

From the yards below the Team Track, train bells rang noisily across the twilight. Above them, a crescent of new moon became visible in the darkening sky. Mike waited tensely for Suleiman to respond.

"I've felt about Greeks the way you felt about Turks," Suleiman said, his voice suddenly grave. "But you're not only one tough little Greek, tough as anyone I've ever met, you're a champion at what you do. I've watched you work, and you're a champion."

Mike was moved by Suleiman's words.

"You could be a champion too!" Mike cried. "I tell you, Suleiman, you've got the stuff! I been icing for a hell of a long time and I know!"

"I'm not an iceman."

"The hell you're not!"

"I don't want to be a damn iceman!"

"I'm telling you, you're a born iceman! "

Suleiman was silent for another moment, and then he shook his head.

"You're really a piece of work," he said. "I got to say I've never run into anyone like you, Greek or anything else." He paused. "Maybe if I'd come here to the Team Track a few years ago, before a lot of other stuff happened—" He shrugged. "It's too late now."

"Maybe it isn't too late," Mike said urgently. "I got to tell you, no matter how many times you turn me down, well, I'm going to keep trying. You got the makings of a champion too, a skill you can pass on . . ." He paused. "Maybe to other Greeks or Turks who come to work at the Team Track."

Suleiman laughed.

"You and I may be the last Greek and Turk to ever step foot in the Team Track."

They started walking slowly through the falling darkness to their cars.

"How did you get started icing?" Suleiman asked.

"I came over from the island of Crete when I was a kid and started washing dishes in my uncle's lunchroom," Mike said. "After the lunchroom, I worked the stockyards for a while and, one day, saw a crew on a HiLift icing the cars. Watching the way they worked blew me away. I came to the Team Track and got a job. That was more than thirty years ago." He paused. "What about you? You born overseas too?"

"In Ankara," Suleiman said. "It's a city in Turkey south of Istanbul that Greeks still call Constantinople. We lived with my parents until my brother and I came over about ten years ago on a labor contract with the Santa Fe. I spent the war years working on a track gang in New Mexico until my contract was up. My brother's still working there."

"Your brother as big as you?"

"Pretty close. I think we got our size from my father, who was a circus strong man. They'd chain him to a full-sized horse, and he'd pull the horse across the ring."

"He must have been a terror."

"He helped toughen my brother and me," Suleiman said. "A light slap from his hand could break your jaw."

"How'd you come to Chicago?"

"After I left the railroad, I worked a few years in a steel mill in Birmingham," Suleiman said. "I got restless and one day I caught a ride into Chicago with a trucker hauling steel plate. I came to the icehouse when I heard they were hiring summer help."

They reached their cars.

"You live around here?" Mike asked.

"I got a room on Roosevelt near Maxwell Street," Suleiman said. "I like the neighborhood. We got a district like it in Ankara called Samanpazari, where old men sit in stalls hammering copper into samovars or selling carpets and costume jewelry for tourists. Here it's hot dogs, and back home its kebob and souvlaki."

"You ever think about going back?"

"What for?" Suleiman shrugged. "People there are poor as hell and don't have enough to eat. There's nothing back home for me any longer."

As Suleiman opened his car door, Mike stopped him.

"Listen, Suleiman—" Mike hesitated a moment and then pressed on. "How about you and me shaking hands? It would be like we're wiping away a thousand years of being enemies, a Greek and a Turk, burying the hatchet without putting it in the other guy's head."

For a moment Suleiman didn't respond, and Mike feared he'd be turned down. Then Suleiman slowly extended his hand. Feeling the Turk's broad palm and strong fingers clasping his own big hand sent a vibration like an electric charge through Mike's body.

"Well, all right then!" he said, and jubilation made his voice tremble. "By God, Suleiman, we'll show them what a Greek and Turk working together can do!"

Sometimes on Saturday mornings, before the day's heat became intense, Mike and Reba took a walk along Maxwell Street. Although she had lived in the neighborhood for years, she'd only been on the notorious street a few times and had found it bedlam. Seeing it with Mike made it, she told him, a new experience.

He showed her Smoky Harry's used clothing store with the sign over the door, WE CHEAT YOU FAIRLY. There was Sam's Tailor Shop with pressing machines that released great clouds of steam into the air.

Mike took her to Sangamon and Fourteenth Place, known, he told her somberly, as "dead man's corner," where more criminals had been shot by police and more police shot by criminals than on any other street in Chicago.

"Were you ever in any of those shoot-outs?"

"You're damn right I was!" Mike said earnestly. "I was right there in the middle of it once with bullets popping all around me! I tell you I had to do some fancy skipping and hopping to keep from being shot in a dozen places!"

She broke into laughter. Then she clasped his arm tightly and they walked on.

In the following few blocks, they saw a man with a dancing chicken on his head, an old lady selling a litter of kittens, and a card artist befuddling his circle of watchers by his sleight-of-hand with a deck of cards.

Reba was impressed with how many of the merchants Mike knew by name, and she was also tickled at the formal way he introduced her.

"This is my wife, Mrs. Dolores Reba Zervakis, who hails from Atlanta," Mike told several of the merchants gravely. After they'd moved on, Reba laughed.

"Where did Atlanta come from?"

"I read about it in a book. The story had to do with plantations in the south and a horny southern girl named Scarlett—"

"That's *Gone with the Wind*! I read that book. Did you read it?"

"Not all of it."

"How much of it?"

"Well, I kind of skimmed a few pages," he confessed. "I'd forgotten the title until you reminded me. But I remember reading about those elegant southern ladies with fine clothes and fine manners who all came from Atlanta."

"What if you introduce me to someone who really comes from Atlanta?" Reba said. "And they ask me where I lived in Atlanta, or my favorite restaurant in the city?"

"Don't you worry about that," Mike reassured her. "If someone I introduce you to turns out to be from Atlanta, I'll get us the hell away from there in a hurry." He winked. "I'll tell them we're late for lunch with the mayor!"

By late in September, summer's sharp edges had given way to the first signs of autumn. In a few flower boxes lodged in the windows of Mike's building, the zinnias and geraniums had begun to fade.

With the cooler weather, the tempo of icing slowed down, as well. In a few more weeks, the last of the summer workers would be gone, and Mike and the other veterans, joined, he fervently hoped, by Suleiman, would get ready for winter.

There was a day in that September when Mike and Billy iced at the Grand Trunk and then drove to service a train in the I.C. yards. As they were finishing, the yardmaster brought them a phone message from Rafer that they should come back in.

"Did he say why?" Mike asked.

The yardmaster shook his head.

"He only said tell you to come right back."

"What you think is up, Mike?" Billy asked.

"I don't know," Mike said. "Maybe there's a rush order for a train that's late."

When they drove up the Team Track hill, Rafer waited for

them outside the office. Mike stopped the truck and Rafer hurried around to his window.

"There's been an accident," he said, his face pale and his voice trembling. "Mendoza . . . he's been hurt."

Mike felt a tightness in his chest.

"What happened?"

"An accident at the CN&W yard," Rafer said. "The yardmaster called for an ambulance that took Mendoza to Emergency at St. Luke's Hospital over on Harrison. Some of the men are with him." He paused for breath. "Earl's inside talking to downtown. They're raising hell about the accident."

"Take the truck in," Mike said to Billy. He swung down from the cab and started for his car.

"I'd come with you, Mike," Rafer said. He gestured toward Earl in the office. "I got to stay here."

Mike drove swiftly to the emergency entrance of the hospital. Inside the swinging doors, he inhaled the strange, oppressive odors he associated with illness and hospitals. Almost at once, he saw Noodles, Stamps, and Suleiman standing in the corridor. He walked quickly toward them, searching their faces for some reassurance that Mendoza was all right.

"Where is he?"

Noodles pointed to an alcove concealed by a long gray curtain.

"They're coming to get him now," he said, his voice low and somber.

"They moving him to a room upstairs?" Mike asked.

For a long moment no one spoke.

"Mendoza's dead, Mike," Stamps said gruffly. "They coming to take him to the dead room."

For a shaken moment, the words clashed against an image Mike had of the invincible young iceman riding the trucks and heaving the ice.

Mike walked to the alcove, pushed the curtain aside, and entered. The small, barren space held only a gurney on which a figure lay covered by a sheet. Mike slowly lowered the sheet and saw Mendoza's face. His head seemed carved in stone, his eyes locked, his cheeks rigid and gray. A small blue vein discolored his temple.

Mike reached out slowly and touched Mendoza's cheek. When he pulled his fingers away, they carried the chill of the death they had touched.

He stared at his friend's still face for a long time, a tangle of emotions rioting in his body. Remorse, sorrow, disbelief that it could have happened, that Mendoza could have started work that morning and within a few hours be dead.

He drew the sheet back over Mendoza's head and walked a little unsteadily from the alcove back to the others.

"What happened?"

"It was an accident, Mike," Noodles said quickly. "You know, just an accident."

"Could have happened to any of us," Stamps said gravely. His eyes were moist and his cheeks wet. "Hell, Mike, you know how close I came to getting killed last year at the Belt Harbor when I slipped off the car . . . I mean, hell, it could happen to any of us."

Mike looked at Suleiman.

"What happened?"

Suleiman stared at him in silence. After a moment, he could no longer meet Mike's gaze and looked away.

"We were icing from moving trucks." Suleiman's voice held a tremor. "His truck hit a bump and he got thrown. A freight was rolling on the other side and . . . he went under the wheels . . ."

In the tight silence that followed, Stamps muttered something under his breath.

"Mike, it wasn't Suleiman's fault," Noodles said earnestly. "Mendoza was pushing him too . . ."

"I'm sorry," Suleiman said, the words low and husky from his throat.

Mike thought how hard he had worked to teach Suleiman to ice, struggled to make him the best, labored to build his skill and prowess. And Suleiman had used all that Mike had taught him to send Mendoza to his death. A knife blade of rage cut into his heart.

"Goddam you!" he said in a low hoarse voice. "Goddam you, Turk, for bringing your cursed blood here. Goddam you for not giving a shit about anyone but yourself! I wish you'd never picked up tongs, never stepped on a HiLift. Goddam you, Turkish bastard, goddam you!"

The curses drained him of breath and his voice broke. He felt the uselessness of words to undo what had been done. He turned then and walked down the corridor to the door.

When he got to his apartment, he told Reba that the young iceman, Luis Mendoza, who had been best man at their wedding, was dead. Afterwards, he went into the bedroom and lay down. He didn't turn on the lamp, but the lights from the signs on Halsted Street flickered across the shadowed ceiling of the room. After a while, Reba came quietly to sit on the edge of the bed. When he was finally able to tell her how Mendoza had died, the words burning his lips, she lay down beside him, her fingers across his chest, over his heart.

"Mendoza and me been icing together for ten years," Mike said. "He was just a boy when he started, but he became a real good iceman . . ."

He paused as he recalled Mendoza on the gurney. In those first moments, seeing him cold and still, Mike had considered only his own loss. Now he thought of the young man's parents, who would mourn him, and the girl in his village who hoped to marry him. Death had robbed them and Mendoza of all the life he might still have lived.

For the first time in as many years as he could remember, he could not control his tears. A strange, torn moaning came from his lips.

He cried because Mendoza was lost forever to the family and friends who loved him. And he cried, as well, for the senseless death of one iceman and for the senseless waste of another.

10

Rafer

THE BEGINNING OF OCTOBER BROUGHT THE city a series of sun-bright days and crisp, cool nights. For the first time in months, Rafer slept with a quilt pulled across his bed. The air seeping in through his open window at dawn carried scents that recalled for him the autumns of his childhood.

Several months had passed since the night he and Leota had lapsed into their bouts of drinking. He had seen her a few days later in the hotel lobby. Uncertain whether she'd still be hurt or angry, he approached her nervously to tell her once again that he was sorry. Pale and withdrawn, she appeared to accept his apology, but she said nothing. The following day, when he asked the hotel clerk about her, he learned she had checked out without leaving any forwarding address. She had disappeared into the vastness of the city, and he'd probably never see her again. Nor would he ever know if she'd succeeded in overcoming her addiction. As for his part in starting her drinking again, that added one more regret to those that already burdened him.

In the cool, clear dawns of that October, Rafer sometimes walked from the hotel to the Team Track. Within a few weeks, his job would be over, and he'd decided he would move on to another city, another way station on his journey to regain his family.

That morning, he walked for perhaps one of the last times through the cluttered neighborhood he had come to know so well. Every third store was a tavern, its shabby window displaying bottles of whiskey and wine with faded labels and threadbare posters of lissome girls in bathing suits smoking Pall Malls or Lucky Strikes.

Set among the taverns were the small ethnic stores. There was the Spartan Barber Shop with an ancient barber's chair that served as camouflage for a back room where old Greek men played cards. There was the narrow Sicilian grocery, its window containing cans of olive oil and jars of black olives. At that early hour, the sidewalk vegetable stall before the store was still covered with canvas. Beside the grocery was the Tijuana lunchroom, the window containing wax replicas of enchiladas and tortillas and a sun-faded painting of the revolutionary leader Emiliano Zapata. On the corner of Jackson and Halsted, scents of wax and incense drifted from the Kalamata candle shop, whose window held votive candles and miniature icons of Jesus, Mary, and the saints.

As he crossed Roosevelt Road, Rafer passed beneath a maze of fire escapes suspended from shabby tenements that housed the new immigrants who moved into the neighborhood. On hot summer evenings, the fire escapes were crowded with families fleeing their stifling rooms. All night long, the wails of heat-afflicted babies floated across the darkness.

At Fifteenth Street, Rafer turned off Halsted. As he walked up the rutted gravel hill, he recalled the cold, rain-drenched night in March when he'd come to the Team Track for the first time.

With the cooler weather, the feverish tempo of summer icing activity slowed down. Rafer continued to work days in the office with Earl while Benny came in to work nights.

Much of the daily routine of work remained the same, yet with Mendoza's death, the Team Track was starkly changed. After the accident, Mendoza's brother had come to Chicago and taken his body back to Mexico. Mike had gone down for the funeral but said nothing about it to anyone when he returned.

The death of their friend darkened the mood of the veteran icemen. Noodles and Stamps were short-tempered, quick to snap, and quick to curse. Sigmund and Thadeus seemed even more somber and impassive, washing up and changing clothes quickly and silently after work and leaving.

The mood of the young summer workers was also darkened. Mendoza had been the veteran closest to them in age, and his death made them aware that youth and strength did not make them immortal.

At the end of the day, there was little of the usual laughter and horseplay in the locker room. The men washed and changed hurriedly, as if anxious to leave. Rafer heard them walking by his office window in small groups, their voices fading into the rumble of old car motors.

Among the young icemen, Suleiman had become a solitary, reclusive figure. In response to whispers among the men that his recklessness and bravado had caused Mendoza's death, anger and defiance had frozen his features so he appeared always to be scowling. Rafer suspected what bothered Suleiman the most was that he knew Mike blamed him for the death of Mendoza.

Yet it was Mike who was most changed. Seeing him in the locker room or in the office, Rafer was shocked at how Mendoza's death had transformed him. The lines of age and weather seemed carved more deeply in his face, his cheeks were darker, his eyes bloodshot. In the midst of others, he remained brooding and withdrawn. Men were wary about speaking to him unless he spoke first. That was true even for Noodles and Stamps, who had been his friends the longest.

In the locker room at the end of the day, Rafer heard stories from men who had iced with Mike during the day in the railroad yards. They spoke with awe of the way he worked with a savage intensity, scornful of others who could not keep pace with him. Day after day, he iced more cars than any other man at the Team Track. The men believed that Mike was driven by his grief at Mendoza's death. Rafer felt that Mike's fury and intensity were driven, as well, by the loss of his hopes and the wasting of his dreams.

As for how Mike regarded Suleiman, at those times Rafer saw

them together in the locker room, Mike never gave the young Turk a glance or a word, treating him as though he didn't exist.

Yet Suleiman didn't display the same resentment and defiance toward Mike he showed to others. Rafer felt that alone among the men at the Team Track, Suleiman understood how much Mike had lost and he seemed anxious to mend the breach between them.

On one occasion, Rafer saw Suleiman approach Mike in the locker room.

"I'm sorry, Mike, I left you that dry potato car at Proviso," Suleiman said in a low voice. "We ran out of ice and had to come back to reload."

Mike looked at him silently, and then he turned brusquely, almost contemptuously, away. Stung by the rejection, Suleiman caught sight of Rafer and, for a moment, the young Turk's face revealed his own raw pain. Then he turned away.

One morning that October, Earl called Suleiman into the office.

"We got a year-round job open," Earl said tersely. "There'll be more money and insurance and medical benefits. But don't take the goddam job unless you plan to stick it out 'til next summer."

"I don't want the job," Suleiman said brusquely. "I'm moving on pretty soon now."

"I didn't want the sonofabitch anyway," Earl muttered after Suleiman left the office. "Downtown is after me to keep him on. Now I can tell them he won't stay."

Whatever grief Earl felt about Mendoza's death was submerged in his resentment because downtown held him accountable. Several times he raged to Rafer and Benny about the accident.

"That goddam Greek is the one to blame! He put those fancy ideas about icing into the men! Mendoza and the Turk would never have tried that shit if they hadn't seen the old bastard showing off! I tried to tell that to downtown, but the sons-a-bitches wouldn't listen!"

Yet Earl was pleased at the schism between Mike and Suleiman. He saw in Mike's brooding and in the compulsive way he worked an opportunity to drive him to quit. Rafer felt the only reason Earl hadn't yet fired the clumsy youth, Billy, was to keep him as helper on Mike's truck, where he'd be more of a burden than a help.

In what Rafer regarded as an even more brutal action on Earl's part, when a single crew had to be called at night to ice a special train, Earl ordered Benny to call Mike first.

Yet Mike accepted every challenge Earl hurled against him. He never refused a night assignment, carried it out swiftly, and, despite his lost sleep, came to work in the morning as if he had drawn upon some wellspring of energy. Rafer felt that if any passion still motivated Mike, it might have been his resolve to win one last battle against Earl.

One evening in mid-October, Noodles and Stamps entered the office after Earl had left. Benny had arrived for the night shift, and Rafer was getting ready to leave.

The two icemen loomed above Benny at his desk. He stared up at them nervously, his tongue emerging to lick his dry lips.

"You called Mike for that special again last night," Stamps said harshly. "Why in hell don't you call someone else?"

"I don' wanna do it!" Benny said shrilly. "I know I could call you guys, but it's Earl," he grimaced. "Earl tol' me always call Mike firs'. Ask Rafer. It ain' my fault if Mike don' say no."

"Maybe you could talk to Mike, Rafer," Noodles said grimly. "Stamps or me or any of a half dozen other guys can take the specials. He won't listen to us, but maybe you could talk some sense into him."

"Mike takes those specials as a challenge from Earl," Rafer said. "He won't back down."

"He's sure one stubborn iceman," Stamps grumbled.

"Goddamit, we have to talk to Earl!" Noodles said vehemently. "Make him understand its not fair!"

"Won't do any damn good," Stamps said scornfully. "That bastard don't have a heart."

After they left the office, Benny looked despondently at Rafer.

"T'ose guys blame me," he said unhappily. "Hones' to God, Rafe, you know it ain' my fault . . ."

"They know it's Mike's choice," Rafer reassured him. "They know all he has to do is say no."

"But he ain' goin' to say no," Benny said slowly. "He ain' goin' to say no 'cause . . . he's Mike . . ."

The following afternoon, Noodles and Stamps returned to the office to stand before Earl's desk, waiting tensely for several minutes until he finally looked up.

"What the hell you doing in here?" Earl snapped. "You should be on your way to the Grand Trunk."

"Trucks are loaded and ready, Earl," Noodles said, "We just need to talk to you a minute first."

Rafer heard anxiety struggling with loathing in Noodle's voice.

"It's about Mike," Stamps said.

"What about him?"

"We don't think Mike should be called out for the specials at night." Noodles faltered and turned to Stamps for support.

"It's not right," Stamps said gruffly.

"What's the matter? Is the old man whining I'm working him too hard?"

"Hell, Earl, you know Mike's not a whiner!" Noodles said indignantly. "But he can't work days and nights too! No man alive can do that." He drew a deep breath. "And that lead-assed kid working with him doesn't help him any."

"Are you telling me how to schedule my crews?" Earl's voice rose.

"Nobody's trying to do that, Earl," Noodles said doggedly. "Hell, everybody knows Mike's the best iceman at the Team Track, but he can't keep working like this."

"Noodles and me will take any special," Stamps glared at Earl. "No damn need to call Mike."

Earl's bulk seemed to swell larger in his chair.

"Who I call in to work is none of your goddam business! If the old man's got a complaint, let him come to me! He won't squawk because he likes the overtime dough! Now, get the hell back to work!"

A growl of rage came from Stamps, and Noodles reached quickly to grasp his arm. He pulled Stamps away from the desk, urging him toward the door. As they left the office, Stamps's angry voice carried back, "I told you wasn't any goddam use!" The door banged closed behind them.

Rafer didn't know how Mike learned that Stamps and Noodles had appealed to Earl. The following evening, after Earl had left, Rafer heard angry voices from the garage adjoining the office. He went to listen just inside the door.

"You had no goddam right to talk to him about me!" Mike's voice rang blunt and angry. "That's my business and mine alone! I'll see the bastard in hell before I ask him for anything!"

"We were only trying to make him understand, Mike," Noodles said, "make him see how crazy it is to keep calling you."

"That bastard don't have a heart," Stamps said. "Somebody needed to talk to him."

"This is between Earl and me!" Mike said. "He knows what the hell he's doing, and I know what the hell I'm doing! You guys back off! Understand?"

Fearful as Rafer was of Earl's anger and despite Mike's demand that no one interfere, Rafer made an effort to help him. Without letting Earl know, he altered the work schedules and reassigned one of the better young icemen to replace Billy as Mike's helper. That subterfuge lasted only until the following day, when Earl checked the schedule.

"Who the hell put Farley on with Mike?" he waved the schedule at Rafer. "Was it you or Benny?"

"I put him on, Earl," Rafer said. He braced himself for Earl's fury.

"Well, all right," Earl said. "I'll leave it that way." A hoarse chuckle came from his throat. "With Farley on his truck, nobody can squawk I'm not giving the old bastard all the help I can."

That baleful tactic by Earl outraged Rafer. It was as if the straw boss understood that Mike's despair and frustration were compelling him toward a calamity no matter who his helper was. In that moment, Rafer despised the straw boss more vehemently than he ever had before.

But the plans of both Rafer and Earl were thwarted the following morning when Farley, the young iceman assigned to Mike, came into the office. He was a tall, strong-bodied youth with a shock of blonde hair. He stood awkwardly just inside the door, looking nervously at Earl.

"Mike don't want me on his truck," Farley spoke in a low, halting voice.

"Why don't he want you?" Earl snapped. "You been fucking up?"

"No sir!" Farley said earnestly. "No sir! That's not it at all! Mike said I work just fine. He just doesn't want me. He wants Billy back." Farley shook his head as if he found that hard to understand. "That's who he said he wanted."

Earl stared at the young man, his jaw working as if he were chewing on pebbles. For several moments he didn't speak, and then he brusquely waved the young man out. Farley left quickly.

"How do you like that sonofabitch!" Earl's voice rang with outrage. "I do him a favor, and he spits in my face! Well, all right then!" He motioned angrily at Rafer. "If that's what the hell he wants, give that useless shit Billy back to him!"

There were times in that month when Rafer, seeking to escape the tension he felt at the Team Track, came close to drinking again. He recalled the moment earlier in the summer when his parched tongue first tasted the wine in Leota's room, and his thirst returned with a fury. But he avoided taking a drink because of his love for his wife and daughter. In some strange way, he also felt that by remaining sober he was redeeming a measure of the guilt he felt about Leota.

There was a Saturday morning in that month when Rafer was working alone in the office. Two crews were icing at the yards, and the only other employee at the Team Track was Salvatore, at work in the garage on the trucks.

Rafer heard a car on the hill and, a few moments later, the

sound of voices in the garage. Then the door from the garage opened, and Mike and Reba entered the office.

Reba was dressed in a print dress and light jacket. Her hair was brushed back and coiled up in a bun, and in a small adornment to her loveliness, she wore a glistening white flower above her ear.

Mike was clean shaven, dressed in tan slacks and a sweater. He appeared tense, his face revealing his aggravation. Rafer rose to greet them.

"I made Mike bring me in to see this famous Team Track for myself, Rafer," Reba smiled. "This place where he's spent so many years."

"I told her there wasn't a damn thing to see here," Mike said impatiently. "Some battered lockers, a mountain of ice, and a garage full of broken-down trucks."

"It's where you work," Reba said. "That makes it special for me." She gestured at Rafer. "He even agreed to let me ride in his truck."

"She made me promise," Mike shook his head. "I think it's nuts."

"I've never ridden in a truck."

"You haven't missed anything. Believe me, hon, it'll shake your guts out. You might even chuck up your breakfast."

"You promised."

"You'll get your dress dirty."

"A dress can be washed. You promised."

"All right, all right!" Mike said in resignation. "I'll take you for a ride. Maybe we'll drive all the way downtown and show off the iceman's limo before the rich yahoos." He gestured toward a chair. "Wait here with Rafer. I'll bring the truck down."

After Mike left the office, Reba sat down across from Rafer. The contrived smile left her face, leaving her looking drawn and pale.

"What do you think, Rafer?" she asked slowly. "You're with him every day. How does Mike seem to you?"

"He's working really hard, Reba."

"It's more than work," Reba said in a low voice. "There's a fever in him that doesn't let him slow down or rest. He doesn't become angry with me, but there's so much anger in him."

"Maybe time will help, Reba, maybe time will work things out."

They sat for a moment in silence.

"What I find the hardest are the nights waiting for the phone to ring," Reba said. "The only calls I remember coming in at two or three in the morning are calls when someone has died."

"He shouldn't be taking those specials," Rafer said. "He could just tell Benny no, and Noodles or Stamps would be glad to take them."

"I know it's his choice, Rafer, and I've begged him to say no. After working all day, it doesn't make any sense for him to work at night. He has trouble sleeping, and he just lies there awake, as if he's waiting for the phone to ring. He says he's got to go . . . something between this man, Earl, and him. He says I wouldn't understand and he's right." She sighed. "I've never understood what men call their pride and all the foolish, absurd things they do in the name of that conceit."

The wail of a siren carried from Halsted Street, its strident sound rising and then fading away. Reba shifted restlessly in her chair.

"I don't really care about the truck," she said. "I wanted to come here so I could see for myself why his bond to this world is stronger than his bond to me. I wanted to see what I had to fight." She paused and shook her head. "I don't understand . . ." she gestured toward the hill outside. "What is it, Rafer? What is there here that Mike fights for so hard ?"

Rafer struggled for an answer. How could he make Reba understand Mike's passion for his work, his resolve not to let Earl break him, his grief at Mendoza's death, or how he felt Suleiman had betrayed him?

As if she understood the futility in his silence, Reba nodded slowly.

"When Mike and I married," she said quietly, "I had this

dream, Rafer, about the two of us living out our lives in a small, frame cottage in the country. There would be white wash on a line in the yard, and I'd learn to bake bread. We'd grow old together and take care of one another."

The rumble of Mike's truck sounded on the hill. Reba rose slowly to leave.

"I should have known that I've lived too wicked a life for a dream like that to come true," Reba said pensively. "I'd pray except I don't think God listens to a whore's prayers. But whatever happens, Rafer, I'll be forever grateful to Mike. When he asked me to be his wife, it was like a grace, a blessing that swept aside all the sad and worthless years."

She paused beside Rafer's desk and he stood up. She stared sadly into his eyes and in a restless, fumbling gesture reached up to take the flower from her hair. She pressed it gently into Rafer's hand.

"Watch out for him, Rafer," she said softly. "Help him in any way you can because I can't help him now."

After she'd left the office, a faint scent of her perfume lingered in the stale, trapped air.

The Saturday after Reba and Mike's visit to the Team Track, Rafer walked to the Pacific Garden Mission Church. He knew how close Israel was to Mike, and he hoped there might be something the preacher could do to help.

He found Israel in the basement room of the mission kneeling in prayer with a small group of homeless men. Rafer sat down and waited. After a while, the men rose and dispersed, drifting slowly toward the door. Israel came to sit beside Rafer. The preacher's eyes appeared heavy-lidded and weary.

"I know, Rafer, you've come about Mike," Israel said quietly. "Reba also came to see me a few days ago. I can only tell you what I told her. I'd give my life for that man, but there's nothing I can do."

"Won't he listen to you, Preacher?"

"He'll listen. He just won't deny what he's doing."

"But driving himself the way he's doing makes no sense."

"If men always acted in a rational way," Israel said gravely, "the history of the world would be starkly different."

They sat for a moment in silence.

"In the chaos and disorder of every age," Israel said slowly, "there are men who hold visions and beliefs with a passion our shallow and selfish society cannot understand. These men carry within them an inner map of the world that belongs only to them. Sometimes they battle for noble causes, for a country's freedom, or to challenge the tyranny of despotic leaders. They endure jail and even death for their beliefs."

Israel paused, one gnarled hand rising to push back his tangled white hair.

"Now, you might ask, what right does this ordinary man, this iceman driving a wreck of a truck, what right does he have to think his life has a mission? But, large or small, noble or ordinary, men like Mike believe they have been entrusted with something of value they must pass on, a task or mission larger than they are. And which of us has the right to say to them that they are wrong or that their battle is useless."

Several shabby old men entered the room and paused near where they were sitting. Israel gestured at them to wait.

"It's hard to admit we can do nothing," Israel said. "We cannot ease for him the burden of Mendoza's death or recover his dream that the young Turk would be his savior. A small man would give up, but Mike only knows how to fight on." Israel sighed. "Those of us who love him can only pray. Will you pray with me, Rafer?"

"I'm not a godly man, Preacher," Rafer said in apology.

"No matter how wretched or sinful he has been, a man who prays will find God's ear," Israel said. "Then God will decide whether that prayer can be answered."

Israel slipped slowly from the chair to his knees, and Rafer knelt beside him. The preacher took his hand, and Rafer felt the preacher's touch as if it were a healing balm. He bent his head and for a trembling moment recovered the untroubled faith of his childhood prayers. He prayed fervently for Mike and Reba, for Mellie and Rosie, for Leota, the woman he had wronged, and, finally, for himself that he might someday be saved.

After a moment, Israel rose slowly, uncoiling his body to his towering height.

"If our faith is strong enough, Rafer, we mustn't despair," Israel said. "Whatever happens may be part of a design greater than we frail humans can understand."

He clasped Rafer's hand a final time and then walked toward the small group of men who waited for him.

In the beginning of November, an early winter storm struck the city. For several days, cold rain battered the streets, the water forming small rivers that ran noisily into the sewers. The Team Track hill became soaked and muddy from the rain, and the motors of the old trucks labored to make the ascent.

The storm moved on, and the muddy puddles dried, leaving behind a smell of wet earth and rotting leaves. There followed a series of lovely, unseasonable days, a final fleeting remnant of autumn before the winter. One afternoon, standing on the Team Track hill, Rafer saw a great flock of birds massing for their migration.

Many of the young summer workers had already left, and most of the rest would be gone in another week. In the locker room at the end of the day, the conversations of those who remained turned on the places they would go when they moved on.

Rafer was grateful because the colder weather meant fewer specials at night for Mike. But it also resulted in Earl's presence in the office for the full day. To escape his brooding silence or his voice haranguing a yardmaster, Rafer spent as much time as he could in the locker room, at day's end mingling with the men who were washing and changing to leave.

On Friday evening of the first week in November, Rafer was in the locker room. Most of the crews had already checked in when Rafer saw Mike enter the room and walk slowly to his locker. He sat down on the bench beside it and rested his back against the wall. When Rafer walked over to him, his eyes were closed. As Rafer's shadow fell across his face, he opened them again.

"How's it going, Mike?"

"All right, Rafe," Mike said, and weariness slurred his speech. He fumbled in his jacket pocket and pulled out a crumpled bill of lading he handed to Rafer. "For those three cars at the I.C."

He leaned back against the wall and closed his eyes once more.

Several men called to Rafer with questions about their final paychecks, and he walked over to answer them. A few moments later, when he looked across the room again, he saw Mike still slumped on the bench.

At that moment, Noodles and Stamps entered the room and started to their lockers, which were close to Mike's.

"Look't Mike sleeping," Noodles laughed. "All this noise and the old iceman takes a nap."

Stamps walked to the bench where Mike lay slumped and bent down, looking intently into his face. He placed his big hand gently at Mike's throat. After a moment he straightened up.

"He's dead," Stamps said.

Rafer heard the words as if they were a hammer blow against his head.

"What the hell you talking about!" Noodles cried indignantly. "You must be nuts! Mike's just sleeping! Give him a shake and you'll see!"

"Goddam, I know a dead man!" Stamps said savagely. "You seen the dead I seen, you'd know too!"

As Stamp's words resounded across the locker room, the voices of the men faltered. A few repeated the word *dead* in shocked whispers. The locker room became eerily quiet. A few men pushed closer, staring in shock as Noodles moved to raise Mike's head.

"Leave him be!" Suleiman's voice rang harsh and loud across the room. He pushed his way roughly through the circle of men and crouched beside Mike. When he straightened up, Rafer saw his face stricken with a raw and stunned disbelief. He seemed to want to speak, but no words came from his lips.

An angry muttering swept the room. Rafer turned and saw Earl standing in the doorway from the office. Every man there knew all Earl had done to bring Mike down, and a wave of fury and revulsion rose against him. A dozen men moved to form a barrier, blocking the straw boss from entering the room.

In that tense, silent moment, Suleiman bent and placed his arms behind Mike's back and beneath his knees. With a mighty heave, he raised Mike's body from the bench and swung him like a great sack of grain over his shoulder. The men around him made way as Suleiman, clasping Mike's legs tightly against his chest, started for the door. He kicked it open and walked out. After a moment, Noodles and Stamps followed, and the other men trailed behind. Only Earl and Rafer were left in the locker room, and when Earl moved to follow the others, Rafer followed him outside.

The sun had begun its final descent, casting a scarlet glow across the Team Track buildings and the row of parked trucks at the crest. In a corner of the still-light sky, Rafer saw the faint sphere of a full moon.

Suleiman carried Mike's body across the gravel road up the hill toward the trucks and the big house. Noodles and Stamps and the other men straggled along in his wake while Earl and Rafer trailed behind.

Halfway up the hill, Suleiman met Thadeus and Sigmund walking down. They stopped and stared in shock at Mike's body. Suleiman never paused and, after a moment, Thadeus and Sigmund joined the crowd moving up the hill.

Rafer followed a short distance behind Earl, who plodded slowly and heavily up the hill. Earl wasn't used to climbing, and several times he paused to catch his breath. Men in the rear of the crowd waved their fists at him, warning him to keep away.

Suleiman carried Mike to the row of parked trucks at the top of the hill. When he reached Mike's truck, Noodles and Stamps quickly joined him. They climbed into the cage of the HiLift and took Mike's body from Suleiman's shoulder and lowered him gently to the floor of the truck.

When Suleiman turned from the truck, the sun flashed fire on the tongs and pick in his hands. He walked briskly to the big house, climbed the ladder to the platform, swung open the freezer door, and stepped inside. A moment later, he came out dragging a four-hundred-pound block of ice. With his pick, he swiftly split the block into several large chunks. He caught the chunks in his tongs and, with a powerful, twisting heave of his shoulders and arms, flung the ice out across the hill.

Rafer and the men watched in a bewildered silence. Earl, standing motionless a short distance behind the crowd, his big body trembling from the exertion of the climb, stared mutely at Suleiman, as well.

Suleiman dragged out another block, split it, and scattered the ice across the hill. The chunks splintered and cracked as they struck the ground. As soon as one block had been cut down, he returned swiftly into the big house for another.

Sigmund may have been the first to understand Suleiman's goal was to empty the big house. The stocky iceman pumped his great fist in the air and bellowed in Polish. An instant later, Thadeus joined him, waving his arms exuberantly, as well, his own booming voice joining Sigmund's bellow.

That explosion of approval from the two stoic icemen set off a barrage of whistles and cheers. The men shouted and applauded Suleiman and jeered and cursed Earl. With each block Suleiman dragged out, split, and scattered, their shouts grew louder.

With his own heart pounding, Rafer waited for Suleiman to collapse before the immensity of what he was attempting to do. But Suleiman worked faster and faster, some fury of emotion providing him a reservoir of strength. With every block he dragged out, cut down, and scattered across the hill, the cries and shouts of the men grew louder and more raucous. Rafer heard his own voice shouting with them.

Standing in the back of the HiLift, Stamps appeared laughing and jubilant, while Noodles waved his long arms in the air and gyrated his lean body in a wild, lopsided dance. Thadeus and Sigmund gestured scornfully at Earl, shouting harsh obscenities at him. Other men taunted and mocked the straw boss, as well.

After a while, the hill became littered with hundreds of chunks and fragments of ice. The ice snared the rays of the descending sun and flashed a rainbow of colors back into the sky.

When Suleiman finished cutting down and scattering the final block of ice, he stood for a moment on the platform. Then he raised his tongs and pick high above his head in a savage and defiant gesture of triumph. The shouts and cheers of the men rose to a deafening roar that rolled like thunder across the Team Track hill.

Suleiman leaped from the platform to the ground. He crossed the hill to the HiLift where Noodles and Stamps waited. He swung up into the cab, started the motor and slowly backed the truck from the row of trucks. Men milled alongside the truck, calling their farewells to Mike.

As the truck and the crowd around it began to slowly descend the hill, further down the slope, Earl turned and began a quick, frantic retreat. In his haste, he slipped and fell heavily to one knee, then floundered for a moment until he was able to raise his bulk again. He continued his desperate, clumsy descent.

As Earl came closer to him, Rafer heard his harsh, labored gasping for breath. Then, in a stunning moment of revelation, Rafer saw Earl's despairing face raw with tears. The straw boss stumbled past, leaving Rafer shaken and bewildered as to whether the Goliath's stony heart had finally been moved to weep for Mike's death.

Earl hurried into the office, and a few moments later, his big car emerged from the garage. With tires screeching, he drove down the hill toward Halsted Street.

A moment later, the truck bearing Mike's body rolled past Rafer. He saw Suleiman's dark, rigid face behind the wheel and in the back of the HiLift, Noodles and Stamps, watchful as sentries, stood vigil over Mike's body.

Later, after the last of the men had gone, Rafer fixed a sign to the office door on which he'd printed in large block letters, CLOSED BECAUSE OF DEATH. As an afterthought he added OF THE ICEMAN, MIKE ZERVAKIS. The phone rang, but he didn't answer.

In that moment, feeling sadness at Mike's death, Rafer was also grateful. Israel's words about God's design being greater than mortals could understand made him aware how in death Mike gained what had eluded him in life. Suleiman's emptying the big house of the last block of ice was an act of homage to Mike and one of defiance against Earl. Rafer wasn't sure whether the straw boss would muster the courage to return to the Team Track, but even if he did, word of his humiliation would have spread to every railroad yard and depot and no man would ever fear him again.

Meanwhile, with a compelling certainty, Rafer knew that Suleiman would remain at the Team Track to take Mike's place. In that way he might absolve his guilt and his betrayal of Mike's trust. When the young men returned at the start of the summer to ice, Suleiman would be there to show them what a man should do and what a man could be.

In the afterglow of the miracle he had witnessed, feeling rejuvenated himself, Rafer sat at his desk and began a note to his wife and daughter.

> Dearest Mellie and Rosie:
>
> I am writing you with the news that I have made up my mind to come home. Whatever battles we still have to fight, we will fight together. I cannot wait to hold you both in my arms.
>
> Love,
> Rafer

He folded the letter and inserted it into an envelope, which he addressed and put into his pocket to mail.

He walked outside and stood in the bright moonlight that glittered across the Team Track. At that moment, the blazing trail of a shooting star cut through the dark sky. Rafer accepted it as a sign that heaven itself was granting the earth a moment of splendor in testament to what had taken place on the hill.

In the sparkle of the star's swift arc, Rafer entered his car and drove down the Team Track hill to go to Reba. He left behind him a terrain so covered by ice that it resembled a moonlit arctic landscape at the pinnacle of the earth itself.

Harry Mark Petrakis is the author of eighteen books, including novels, memoirs, and collections of short stories and essays. He has twice been nominated for the National Book Award in Fiction, and his work has appeared in the *Atlantic Monthly, Harper's Bazaar, Playboy, Mademoiselle,* the *Chicago Tribune,* and the *New York Times.* In 1992, he held the Kazantzakis Chair in Modern Greek Studies at San Francisco State University. For the past forty years, he has also been a lecturer and storyteller, often reading his stories to college and club audiences in the old bardic tradition. He and his wife, Diana, live in the Indiana Dunes overlooking Lake Michigan. They have three sons and four grandchildren.